D1576399

THIS JANUARY TALE tells how the people of England endured the aftermath of the Conquest in 1066.

It is not a book about knights or kings. It is a story of the ordinary folk and what it meant to them when a foreign army drove its way across their land, killing, dispossessing and destroying, in an age when only the wealthy ever stood very far from hunger and want.

At its centre is the city of Exeter. For months its people watched the progress of the Normans from a distance, hoping that they would not try to push so far west. Like all other hopes in that terrible year it proved futile. The city was besieged, the walls broken, the followers of Harold and the Godwins driven into exile across the dangerous winter sea.

BRYHER

THIS JANUARY TALE

LONDON

SECKER & WARBURG

First published in England 1968 by
Martin Secker & Warburg Ltd
14 Carlisle St, London W.1

Printed Photolitho in Great Britain by
Ebenezer Baylis and Son Ltd
The Trinity Press, Worcester, and London

FOR HELEN

Foreword

The popular but incorrect view is that Norman culture in 1066 was superior to that of England. Actually the contrary is true. The epoch of Edward the Confessor was overcivilized, the English preferred art, learning and farming to the use of weapons. King Harold had difficulty in keeping an army together. Normandy had been devastated by wars before and at the beginning of the Duke's reign. His soldiers were restless, probably often hungry, and a danger to their ruler till he could find lands for them.

The historian, Stenton, says in his *Anglo-Saxon England*, "It can at least be said that for the ordinary Englishman who had lived from the accession of King Edward to the death of King William, the Conquest must have seemed an unqualified disaster." What is there to add to these words other than to underline a few facts? There can have been hardly a family in the country who did not lose all or most of their land to a foreign intruder. Hundreds of English went into exile, some to join the Varangian Guard, others to Ireland, the North or France. Art and learning virtually disappeared. A magnificent language was largely destroyed, we have to learn the words of *Beowulf* today as if they were a foreign tongue. There is economic evidence that a hundred years after the Conquest many estates were supporting fewer cattle and men. The free peasant of King Edward's time lost his stature and became bound to the soil.

One of the best ways to understand some of the conditions of that age is to read *The Medical Background of Anglo-Saxon England* by Wilfrid Bonser. It is a grim record of survival when there were constant epidemics and little medical knowledge. The book suggests that there may have been a possibility that the immense slaughter of cattle at the time of the Conquest resulted in the introduction of leprosy into England. The ways of life have altered during the last nine hundred years but the basic emotions of human nature change slowly, if at all. What happened, not to the leaders, but to the ordinary people of that time when loyalty to a leader was the basis of morality?

Some say that history does not repeat itself and others say that we were lucky. 1940 almost followed the pattern of 1066.

1056

I

The morning had brought him out. He liked the clear beginnings that only June had when the gray sky crinkled into a rose colored hollow at its edge like the shells he had so often kicked into the water on his native beaches. His weapons were clean, he was free till the muster at noon, and there was enough space for wandering without a farmer shouting at him to be careful of the crops.

A bird whistled. It startled him for a moment with its peevish sound like the "El-dred! El-dred!" that had called him back so often as a boy to watch the fire at the forge. Oh, if he never reached his father's rank nor beat out the perfect weapon that was every smith's dream, he was thankful that he had run away from Exeter and home. He had taken nothing with him but a bag of dried meat and a sharp knife. "The luck of it . . . the luck of it . . ." he said the words aloud. Two years of marching and a winter campaign as hard as any man could desire had not dulled the triumph of having talked his way (he agreed they had been short of men) into the housecarls of Earl Harold's own troop.

Some people clung to life. Yet unless it were perilous what meaning had it for a man and where was life but here, striding through this green world with occasionally a ragged, scarlet flower, up to the sweet, short grasses of the moor and asking only that the sun would soon beat on his shoulders until his senses were as alive as its heat, not only now but until the moment when his doom fell (as it would whether he were a housecarl or a smith) and that he would never again be the dull, reluctant creature saying yes and no, not as he wanted but as was expected of him, coaxing the flames to the point that his father required. Perhaps existence did not seem unbearable to the churls who tramped up and down the furrows without a glance at the long, flowing hills that at this hour of the day had the color of stones. They accepted it because they had never known anything else. He was aware of happiness precisely because these moments counted, tomorrow he might be lying face downwards in a valley with an arrow through his back but he would know what he had lost; there were no riches like experience, he would have lived his life and been conscious of his death.

The moors were clear and he was too near the camp to fear an enemy although the grasses were up to his knees and their heavy seed-pods brushed against his leggings. Unless he had misjudged the distance in this early light, he ought to reach the top of the nearer hill before it was time to return. His companions were certain that there would be no marches until after the harvest but he felt, by the same process, he supposed, that the bees knew which flowers they needed, that something was afoot and that this might be his last opportunity for a time of a few hours alone. After three years as a forge boy, he was still in love with his own freedom.

The grass grew shorter the higher he climbed. It was full of tiny, yellow stars from some creeping wort and a tall green plant whose name, he was no leech, he did not know. The white clouds were beginning to tumble across the sky, it would be a very hot day. Perhaps the one advantage of life at Exeter had been that the city was a port. Sailors from as far away as Brittany and Flanders had brought their tools and weapons to his father to be mended or resharpened and, while they waited, had shared their news. They might know there why Alfgar had been banished but it seemed as if it took a generation before a man heard what was happening fifty miles away in these remote valleys. All they knew was that Alfgar and the Irish had joined the King of North Wales. How surprised they must have been when Earl Harold had attacked them in the middle of the winter but the uneasy peace that had been made had blown away with the April winds. Something was in the air. Poor Godric! He thought he knew what was in his commander's mind. The man had been too long on the border. It was not his fault that they had been assigned to the rearguard during the campaign and left, as a result, on guard in this frontier village. Rumors had reached them that Earl Harold might be coming to Hereford again and if Godric could capture a Welsh chief, he might be rewarded with the farm he coveted. It seemed as foolish to want land as a forge but if a man grew old and his shoulders stiffened, perhaps the sharpness went from the other senses as well. Oh, how he prayed that this might never happen to him.

Of course, they would never defeat the Welsh. They slipped over the river, drove the cattle away from some surprised and undefended farm and were back in their own hills before the housecarls could follow them. Neither Godric nor his comrades knew much about the origins of the dispute, it had gone on as long as anyone could remember but what did it matter? If a man took reasonable care, it was seldom that he got hurt. Except in the winter campaign, and that had been fought along the low lying fields, he had never seen a dead Welshman. Whatever victory either side won, it would go on as Godric said, as long as there were farms one side and mountains on the other.

He was a little out of breath because he had raced in a straight line up to the summit of the hill. They had begun cutting the hay, he saw, in the sheltered meadows near the water. It was a good life, yet in spite of the summer scents and the grass seeds that had stuck to his legs through the dew, his mind leaped back to the winter morning when he had stood among his comrades to pledge his loyalty. His eyes had followed Godric, standing in front of them in a new cloak the color of a russet apple (what strange thoughts come into a man's mind if he has to stand motionless) past the other housecarls and the untidy, straggling farmers called out with the fyrd, up the rise to the polished axes of the bodyguard and the figure, so far away it was only an outline, standing on top of a small rise under the great, golden folds of the banner. Would he ever forget the shout when they had yelled their loyalty, at a signal from their commanders?

If he were offered a manor, if he were offered a house in Exeter, he would not take them. He did not even want to be Godric with the responsibility for thirty under him. He wanted to be what he was, until his doom came to him, the Earl's man and a housecarl in his army.

"But why was Alfgar banished?"

"Who knows? We're a long way from Westminster."

"And the Irish Court."

The day was unusually hot. Godric had been merciful for once and had dismissed them after weapon inspection, but the sultriness had made the men thirsty and bad tempered. They did not know what to do with the extra hours on their hands, unlike the farmers they were not bound to the fields, and they strolled down the road in twos and threes, saying the same things over again that they had already discussed for weeks, without expecting an answer. The big Fair was not until Midsummer but it was market day and a few old women sat behind half empty baskets of greens. A surly peddler had tethered two lean mountain ponies to a post. He seemed too sleepy even to shout to the passers-by and stood silently beside his beasts, staring at the ground from under the brim of a greasy hat, covered with black flies.

"I thought we had taught them a lesson last winter."

"Whatever rumor you've heard, it's only someone somewhere who has stolen a horse."

A cloud of dust blew over them as a wagon lumbered

7

by, a woman with a hen under her arm stopped to greet an old man sitting on a stool, they could see some logs smoldering under a pot through an open door but otherwise the village was quiet, as if its inhabitants were too drowsy to speak.

"Aie!" A yell that could have been heard in the hills echoed beside them. "You were listening to us, were you?" Alwy, a man whom Eldred had always disliked, clutched an urchin by the hair and then shifted his grasp to the boy's throat.

"Oh, Alwy, drop him!" The child's face was turning purple as the housecarl swung him to and fro. "He'll suffocate."

"I'll teach this scum to try and discover our plans."

"How can he understand you if he is Welsh? Hand him over to Godric if he has done something wrong."

"I can deal with him myself."

"Give him a clout and let him go, he's just a child."

Alwy's fist came down on the boy's cheek, he flung him into the gutter where the urchin lay, too stunned to move. The sight of his sprawled body angered Alwy who was obviously drunk, and he stooped to give his victim a second thrashing.

"No," Eldred jerked away the already lifted arm, "whatever he's done, you've punished him enough." As answer, the housecarl snatched the knife that they all wore at their belts and turned on his comrade.

Eldred was as quick. He stepped to the side, dodging the thrust and before Alwy could recover his balance, he would have plunged a dagger into his opponent's arm if Godric had not knocked the knives aside with his heavy staff. "You are paid to fight for the Earl and not each other."

"But he was listening when I was telling Oslaf about the new path over the border!" Alwy rubbed his wrist where the stick had caught it.

"And I have ordered you never to discuss it in the open street. Besides, I doubt if that wretched child could understand a word of Saxon," Godric glanced round but somebody had helped the boy up and he had disappeared. "We have given our peace to the people coming to this market and we need their supplies. If you suspected him, the proper thing to do was to bring him to me. As it was your duty, Eldred," he turned on him angrily, "to have fetched your commander before taking to your knives."

His comrades were furious with him. He was certain that Godric had planned a raid (and was probably glad to have the incident as an excuse) but for three days they had grumbled, "What did the boy matter, Eldred? If you hadn't started that scuffle we should have been here for another week," but it was useless telling them they were due to move when he had no proof. Silence was the only weapon at such a moment but after a day's work, a man wanted to sit beside his fellows in the evening, he did not want to be alone. What made it worse was that they knew he would rather be "out," tramping all over those low, heather covered hills, than practicing axe swings and shield grips on a dusty meadow. Yet what was the good of so much formal training when the Welsh fought as archers or by creeping up and stabbing a man in the dark? They had never stood up, as far as he remembered, to a straight attack by the housecarls but melted away if sighted, as if they were not men but creatures of their own mist.

He strolled along the river bank under the pretext of looking for a special twig that was useful for polishing straps. Soon it would be Midsummer and even he hoped that they would be back for the feast. How sluggish the water was! They had not cut the rushes back sufficiently the previous autumn. Still, they looked like swords, beautiful shapes but too soft, he smiled at the memory, for a forge. A clump of marsh iris in their midst had already flowered. He sat down and was about to undo his belt when a scuffling noise startled him and he turned so sharply that he almost upset a basket of eggs that a boy was carrying towards him. "For you," it was the urchin that Alwy had almost suffocated, "they have just been laid."

"So you speak Saxon?" Had Alwy been right, was the boy a messenger sent to find out which was the path that they would take into the hills?

"Only a few words." He answered slowly as if trying first to find the right term in his mind. "I was listening but I am not your enemy. You promised peace to us inside the village but he would have killed me if you had not stopped him."

Eldred was about to answer, "We do not kill children," but altered this hurriedly to "Do you live here?" so as not to hurt the boy's feelings.

"My father lives beyond the border but my grandmother is here and she is ill. She wanted to see me again before she dies."

"What is your name?" In spite of the marks left by Alwy's fist and the burs sticking up from the dark hair after his recent crawl through the undergrowth, something about the boy seemed familiar. Had he seen him before? No, then it came back suddenly, on one of those first dreadful days when he had not dared to leave the forge although his companions had gone berry picking, a young Welsh sailor had brought a knife to be resharpened and had tossed him a penny. He had kept the coin for a long while, it was five times the price that his father would have charged and he ought to have refused it. Only the coin had been in places far away from Exeter and just to hold it had given him a feeling of distance and adventure.

"Kynan." The boy seemed reluctant to answer.

"Ky-nan?" These Welsh words were difficult to pronounce, "But I've heard that name before."

"One of my ancestors was a chief. I was going to stay here till after the Midsummer feast," he paused in obvious disappointment, "but now my grandmother is frightened and is sending me home tomorrow. Eat them, they are not poisoned," he pushed the basket of eggs into Eldred's hand with the mischievous grin of any youngster eager to tease his elders while appearing outwardly polite, "she sent them to you with her blessing."

"Thank her but say I only did my duty." Yet if he were honest, what had it been other than a sudden impulse of a man idly fishing a drowning puppy out of the water? He knew that some of his comrades filched extra food from the weak and elderly; he did not do so himself but he had made no effort to prevent it.

"Most of you do not care but you protected me, you are my brother." There was obviously no difference in Kynan's eyes between the tall, blue eyed Saxon in front of him and his own small, untidy self.

"I am sorry you will miss the feast but I do not trust Alwy. You will be safer with your father." Alwy! What had he said? The man was always drunk and picking quarrels but he was one of the band. What right had he to say a word against him to a Welshman?

"I am leaving with the peddlers at noon."

"With the peddlers?" But by then the housecarls would be on the march themselves and if Alwy saw the boy again on the road he might find some way to take his revenge. Yet to warn Kynan was perhaps to betray his companions although by the time they had finished the beer that they were already drinking heavily on the common, the whole village would know that they were off on some expedition. "Not at noon, Kynan, do you understand?" He felt as if he were still standing at the forge with no way out from what was virtual imprisonment. "Leave tomorrow at the earliest light and don't tell even your grandmother that I warned you."

It was wild country. The base of the hill was covered with brambles but he was alone and free. The thorns broke off harmlessly against his thick leggings, he paused between two clumps of bracken to listen for any scuffle that might betray a Welshman near him, and from the rims of his ears to the toes that he was careful not to dig into the ground, he waited, snuffling the scents of a summer day as profoundly and eagerly as a hound. Godric had intended the task to be a punishment, instead it was an unexpected gift. "Find out if they are using the upper ford again, Eldred, and then rejoin us as quickly as possible." Why, the man was crazy! Long before the housecarls as a body could struggle through this wilderness, the Welsh would have driven their beasts in safety to the mountains and would watch them from behind the upper rocks, laughing and nudging each other, as the Saxons cut their way upwards, slowly through bushes and gorse.

He rolled over on one shoulder and wriggled round a particularly tough bush. A small oak faced him in a clearing and he paused; there was no sign that the undergrowth had been hacked or the thistles chopped down but it was a place that the Welsh might have used for some of their rites. They might do penance if a wandering priest caught them worshiping a tree but even those who listened to his sermons if they brought in some cattle to a fair, tied ritual offerings to the branches in the hope, he supposed, of gaining a double protection. Scratch the little hornets, as he and his companions called them, and they broke into strange, mournful cries that were more like evocations than prayers.

Oh, they were a dirty and a vicious folk, he would never forget the courtyard in an outlying farm that they had reached too late where the body of an old woman was doubled up among the slaughtered fowls. It had been sheer cruelty, she could not have harmed them. Yet he could understand that they wanted to keep their land, that they struggled with every weapon they had against the Saxon armies that burned their heather and drove them nearer and nearer to the cliff edge and the sea. It was natural for a man to defend the place of his birth. Besides, there was a royalty about the wilderness; those pools in the clefts between the mountains were a deeper emerald than the brooch on the Earl's cloak when they had sworn obedience to him on the previous Christmas feast.

He had seen the ford from the top of a tree earlier in the day. The distance was less than a quarter of a mile but he would have to make a half circle to approach it if he kept to these bushes. There, to the left of the oak, there was the trace of a path. It was overgrown with scrub as if it had been a long time out of use. He listened, a bee was buzzing in the bramble flowers, otherwise the place was utterly still. "Keep to the bracken," Godric had said twice but he knew the dangers better than his commander who had never left the protection of the troop. It was a fool's journey, there would be no traces left at the ford, he was getting impatient. All the same, and he said the names of his companions very slowly over to himself so as not to be precipitate, he would have heard a rustle by now if there were "hornets" in the neighborhood. He paused, parted the bushes and began to crawl towards the path, across the open ground. Five, six movements perhaps and he would be in safety again, he smelled dust, grass, the thick, crumbled pastiness of a bit of bark. Everything depended upon precision, upon knowing what he wanted to do and doing it. . . .

An arrow struck the arm that was pushing him forward but he never heard the drawing back of the bowstring in the thicket.

———

His head was mercifully in shadow but by the middle of the afternoon he would be lying in full sunlight. At the moment he was cold, the cold of the slain that they talked about around the winter fires. The arrow had gone through his arm a little above the elbow and he saw that he had not the strength to pull it out. The pain prevented him from thinking; in a confused way he felt himself responsible. "Never cross a clearing in the open"—it was the first rule that they learned out on the hills. Then everything darkened again, all he could think about was water, a spring, the ford, water tumbling over rocks, springing in a white curtain into the air, rushing into his mouth until he could drown in it, what was that whimpering, it must be some little animal that had also been wounded by an arrow, he was sorry for it until in some shadowy and unfamiliar way he realized that it was his own voice. Water, if he could drag himself to the stream . . . but he was pinned to earth, part of earth, was the freedom for which he fought to be denied him at the last moment? "No man's doom is his own choice," but that was just a saying round the fire, he had never expected it to be true. He tried to rise, to drag the arrow from the turf in which it had partly buried itself but it merely tore the wound so horribly and painfully that darkness flowed over him again, as suffocating as smoke when he longed for the taste of rain.

It was almost noon. If Eldred had been conscious he might have seen a tiny movement above the jagged bracken and, but this was less certain, a worn band of fur where a cap showed between the fronds. He would have grown tired of waiting before a figure crept forward, pressing the grass into the ground as lightly as a hare, to reach the wounded man. Perhaps he would have strained his head sideways to watch Kynan listen until, reassured there was no other watcher, with a speed and strength few would have expected in so young a boy, he cut part of the shaft away and pulled the rest of the arrow from the arm.

Eldred heard himself shriek, then he lost consciousness again and it was not until Kynan tightened the band of linen that he was winding up to the shoulder, that he opened his eyes. "Don't speak, don't move," Kynan glanced anxiously over his shoulder, "it's bad but it could be worse."

Eldred managed to sit up although the pain contracted with each turn of the bandage and he wanted to vomit. He was loosed from the earth, he could move his limbs except for his elbow, the oak stood in the same place, the bushes were unchanged. Flies had come and he brushed one from his forehead with his good arm, but his lips were too dry to form a word. "Can you walk?" Kynan tied a final knot and stood up, "If the man who shot you comes back for your weapons, he may kill us both."

Sometimes a more than natural strength comes into a man. Eldred knelt, he heaved himself up from the ground with Kynan's aid but he had to lean on the boy's shoulder as they crept past the tree and along the almost over-grown track that he had noticed earlier. Words kept going round in his brain as if they were a whisper from some winter world, "Tread lightly, try not to break that twig, keep to the left." He heard breathing, could that rattle possibly be his own, they came out of the woods in front of a shallow bank, he struggled, pulled by Kynan, a few paces more, was he not one of the Earl's men, had he not boasted that he had often burned himself at the forge and that pain meant nothing to him, only now the country was hazy in front of his eyes. "Kneel!" Was that a command? "Kneel!" A hand forced him downwards till he sprawled on the gray and white pebbles, till the stream splashed into his face from a rock and flowed into his face as if from a fountain.

"They were men from another valley and they saw you leave the camp this morning but one of them said he saw a disk on the Saxon's cap and I remembered you were wearing one. Can you follow me a little further? I can hide you in a cave for a few days but we must get there before they come to water the cattle."

"You are sure you are able to walk?" Kynan looked at him so doubtfully that Eldred began to wonder himself. The fever, he thought, was due more to impatience than the wound. His arm ached, that was natural but it was the alternating moments of what felt like sunstroke with intervals of extreme cold that made him long to cross the border and rejoin his companions. Osbern, their leech, made a drink from bothen and old wine that cleared even an infected cut if taken every evening on nine successive days. Besides he was angry with himself for trembling every time he heard a rustle in the bushes and for having slid behind a rock in a fold of the cliff (how ashamed he was of this) when Kynan, bringing back the water that morning, had knocked the jug carelessly against a stone. "How far did you say it was?" The housecarls had marched up one valley and down another till he had no idea if the frontier were hours or days away.

"It is a night's journey to where some of your companions have made a camp."

"Why are you doing this for me?"

"You saved me. It is my duty." Kynan looked up in such surprise that it was clear he thought that Eldred's mind was wandering again.

"Many people would have forgotten." What would he have done himself if their positions had been reversed? "If your own people find you with me, they may kill you."

The boy shrugged his shoulders. "If you really feel strong enough," he looked at Eldred hopefully, "it's a favorable night with a full moon."

"I am ready." He had no bundle, nothing but his knife and as Kynan had often left him to get news or food, he had stared for three days at the damp wall of the cave till he knew every fissure, from the tiny fern that had seeded itself in a hollow near the door to the lopsided boulder at the corner. "This stuff is better outside, it smells of salve." Kynan swept a pile of dirty bracken together and tossed it into the ravine. "Keep your head down." They crawled down the slope into a wood and looking back at the place that had sheltered him, it occurred to Eldred that he would never find the cave again. The base was bracken rising to moorland and rocks but each hill was exactly like the other.

The night was long. It was more and less difficult than Eldred had feared. His fever rose, the brambles round him turned into armed men, their faces laughed at him in the moonlight but turned into branches as he approached them. A blight prowled over the things he loved, everything seemed about to end, in a clash of soundless blades, in a warrior with a spear thrust through the leg that was merely a grim, unburied root of ivy when he came to it, in an archer's grimace from the hollow of a tree. He heard a spatter of paws over the dark decay of leaves, heard Kynan whisper, "Even the cats prefer the open country to this," without understanding what "this" meant, all he could do was to follow his guide through a world full of mist. Ending, ending, what was ending? What were these battle sights that he noticed round him but which his companion seemed not to see? Was it the doom of the world? Why did he keep saying to himself, The berries will rot, there will be no paths for the swine to dig for acorns, family will be set against family for countless generations. What had that arrow taken from him besides the two holes that festered near his elbow? Had the weapon poisoned his brain as well as his mind?

The light was coming into the sky. Kynan kept looking backwards and urging him to a speed beyond his strength. They left the wood and, to his surprise, stepped into the open without any attempt at concealment. "There!" The boy pointed and he saw some hundreds of paces away, the flicker of a fire and the gray, faint outline of a shield.

"Your comrades." Kynan looked away instead of directly at his face as a Saxon would have done, yet now that the parting was near, Eldred felt his rescue was due to friendship as much as duty. It was improbable that they would see each other again and yet it was this Welsh boy with his grimy face and tangled hair who had saved him from a slow, tormented death. He would never have had the strength to pull the arrow from his arm nor, feverish as he was, have found the way back afterwards. "My father forged this knife," he tried to unstrap it from his belt with his uninjured arm, "the Breton captains used to come and buy his work."

"I will not take your father's gift from you."

"It's a remembrance, nobody will know if you make another sheath for it," but Kynan shook his head. Imperceptibly a gulf was beginning to form, perhaps because the indistinct shapes of the men lying under their cloaks round the fire had reminded him of Alwy. "Sometime there may be peace between Earl Harold and your King and if so, come to see me."

"I will come." Kynan pushed the hair back from his forehead and looked straight at the housecarl. "Go to the camp now and join your people. The sooner they attend to your wound the better. We have famous leeches," he looked as proud as if he were leading a Welsh army, "but I dared not take you to them. Farewell, I shall remember you." He disappeared into the wood behind them before Eldred had time to shake his hand or say a word.

It was not yet dawn. Everything was quiet. Some things, separation and thirst, were common to all people, Saxon or Welsh, but in a moment he would be safely inside the tight comradeship of the troop. Osbern would come with his basin and his salves to reassure him about his arm, even Godric would want to know how he had fared, they would ask him if he had loitered with a girl in the thickets but there would be safety even in their jokes and the terrifying visions of the journey would vanish. "It's Eldred," he shouted as he got within hailing distance of the man on watch, "don't shoot, I've had enough of arrows, it's Eldred . . ." and then they were round him, protecting him with just being there and fetching him water to quench his thirst.

He knew this landscape better than his own thoughts. It was the exact rise where he had stopped to look back at Exeter three years previously on his flight to join the Earl's men. The oak sapling that he had noticed then was still growing in the middle of the hedge but it was leaning to one side and he wondered why the farmer had not transplanted it? Still sometimes neither trees nor men survived being moved.

"It is the left arm," he had said to Godric.

"It may be, Eldred, but you cannot swing an axe."

Yet it was just the elbow that was stiff, he could hold a knife on a block, strap the bridle on a mountain pony if the beast did not wriggle too much, he had never run faster and he had his right hand for a sword. Besides, as he had said so often, when had they ever stood in formation on the border?

"Take the Earl's gift and be grateful." Godric had looked away enviously across the fields and he had known precisely what his commander had been thinking. The gold piece was enough to buy a piece of land. "You won't have to crawl through damp grass any longer with the chance that the next arrow will find your heart and not your arm."

A man could pay too great a price for mere life. To quit the Earl's service meant leaving the troop, the grumbling and the gaiety of his companions; it meant being alone and having to accept the bonds of a narrow community to which he had never belonged.

"There is no room for a cripple on the border." It was the same sharp tone that Godric always used if a man had not noticed that the leather grip on his shield was wearing loose and it was envy that had made his commander want to hurt him. "What more do you want? You will be able to live freely on your own farm."

He had almost answered, Take the coin and buy yourself some fields but leave me to take my chance with my comrades in the next raid. Only it would have led to a useless humiliation. Once Godric had made a decision, he would no more alter it than fall back from a position where the Earl had ordered him to make a stand. So he had taken the gold, sold his weapons and slipped away while his companions were out on the border; he had felt disgraced and did not want their sympathy. He moved his elbow with the slightly compulsive gesture that had become a habit and wondered if there were a good leech at Exeter? He trusted Osbern but there was always a possibility that the man had been mistaken. Perhaps the muscles were less torn than he supposed?

Now the moment was near when he would have to face his father. It had nagged him like a toothache throughout the month of his journey. He was near enough to see the walls of the city and the woods where the children picked berries in the autumn. There was time, it was barely midafternoon but he was too restless to sit longer on this bank. He needed to move, to strike something with his fist. Yet the moment he stepped onto the path below him the unity of life was over, the wild cat crouching in the bracken, the smell of a peat fire, the bond of the Earl's service. He would be alone until he died, always alone, not because the arrow had destroyed his weapon pride but because he could never swing an axe again with both his arms.

1067

II

Oh, Elfleda, do you need that other log?" Why was it so difficult to convince people that every scrap of timber, a splinter from a board, a knot cut out of a piece of wood or a small, crooked twig, was as valuable as bread at this particular moment? His wife was a careful housekeeper but she seemed to need an endless succession of fires. He pulled his hood over his head because it was cold and looked mistrustfully at the cauldron.

"Yes, Eldred, if you are really going to walk to Ulgar's farm to see the sword his father left him, it will be late before you return and I have linen I must wash before Christmas. It's chilly now but the sun will be out by midday and I may not have another opportunity before the feast. You know I never waste fuel." Her husband was often irritable; it was something that a wife had to accept like a snow flurry in spring or that sudden truce in the weather in January when the sun shone for a day as if it were April. "If you happen to pass old Alfhelm's cottage, I need a new basket badly and I have not seen him lately at the market."

"Very well but see the boy does not leave. He has work to do and I don't want him wandering off to the town." He knew from his own experience the tricks that an apprentice could play, sliding off on the pretense of taking a mended knife back to its owner and exchanging flakes of iron (fitted to a horn or wooden handle these were excellent for peeling vegetables) for an egg or a honey cake.

"I always look after the house." The times were making Eldred so restless. Nothing that she ever did now pleased him. She must pray at Christmas that the New Year would be less difficult, he had been moodier than ever since he had heard of King Harold's death. Not that he had ever been easy; she watched him stride down the street with the cloak that she had woven for him drawn tightly round his left side because the wind often started his elbow aching again but with his right arm free, and wondered if she had been right to marry him? Her father, before he died, had forced the match on her to safeguard what was left of her dowry. Eldred tried to be affectionate in his way but a woman needed more from life than courtesy and sometimes indifference. Of course she was going to use the time when the forge was unlikely to send a flurry of smuts over everything in the yard to wash some clothes. She picked up two twigs and balanced them against each other, one was thicker and would make a better blaze but the other was oak and would burn longer. It was one of the few joys she had to watch the linen hanging limply at the start, to dry into a smooth, almost wooden texture before evening.

In the afternoon, she thought almost maliciously how Eldred would disapprove, she would walk across to Queen Gytha's hall and ask if she might take Goda home for an hour. The girl missed her companions. It was unusual for a smith's child to have the same training as the family of a thane and she knew that he had paid heavily for the privilege. He was fanatically devoted to the Godwins but there was also a mutual dislike between his stepdaughter and himself. Ought she to have stood up to him at the beginning? Goda was her child, not his. The Queen had lost three sons in the battle and the hall was a gloomy place for one so young. Besides, there were people even inside Exeter who would rather accept Duke William than see their lands harried. If only Eldred would understand that to serve a defeated family might end in difficulties for them all if, and she prayed this might never happen, the city made a bargain with the Normans.

Everything was in its place, the fire was beginning to burn, at least there was not the necessity for saving and scraping that there had been with her first husband. Poor Uhtred! He had been so gay and her father's choice as well but he had believed any story that he heard in the alehouse and most of her dowry had gone buying a. farm with water-logged fields that they could not sell and that had now gone back to moorland. A woman ought to be free to choose the man she married, she had to live with him most of her life.

Well, work was a healer. If only she could get rid of

her fears as absolutely as this dirt that she was rubbing out of a cloak! If . . . people seemed to walk along a narrow line with happiness one side and disappointment the other. What was that? She heard footsteps on the cobblestones, someone was running across the yard and before she could wring out the cloth in her hand, the door was flung open and banged against the wall.

"Goda! Whatever are you doing here in the middle of the morning?" She straightened the blue cloth (it matched the girl's eyes) that was flopping back over her daughter's hair. "I was coming over this afternoon to see if they would spare you for an hour."

"Oh, Mother, let me come home." She looked thin and younger than her fifteen years and had obviously been crying.

"It is only for a year."

"I'm so lonely. They pray and pray and I hate them all."

"Goda! You must not speak of your mistress in that way, she has lost her three sons and a kingdom."

"She sits like a stone and never speaks. Besides, why should I have to stand beside the Lady Gunhild for hours and hours to pick up a thread in case she drops it? I'm not learning embroidery that way nor cooking either. And the prayers! We were three hours in that cold church yesterday and look at my hands . . ." she held out her red and swollen fingers.

"I'll get some fat to rub on them." It was no life for a happy, active girl; besides, Goda was too old. A thane's daughter would have gone to the palace before she was ten and grown up there. "Finish your year and, I promise you, you shall come home."

"I'm not going back," Goda drew her sleeve across her face and sniffled, "it's my stepfather, all he wants is to get rid of me."

"Be quiet, Goda, you are the only girl in Exeter to be trained in the Queen's household." Yet it was true that Eldred had resented the feeling of youth in the house, the girls from the neighborhood running in and whispering together, all the laughter that his own stern father had denied him as a child. Yet each age needed its growth, you could not teach a puppy that could barely stand on its legs how to chase a hare.

"I am learning nothing, the women pray and the men hunt."

"We must all learn patience." She had had to learn, first with Uhtred and his foolish schemes, then with Eldred and his silence. She tried to crush the thought out of her mind but the happiest time had been the years of her widowhood when she had lived alone with her father and her little daughter.

"My father would never have put me there." It was Goda's great weapon. "He might have put me with Dame Mildburh for a time but I think he would have kept me at home."

"You must be obedient, Goda, but I will walk back with you," she glanced in dismay at the pile of wet linen in her basket, "and ask them to excuse you. It is less than a week to Christmas and they promised to let you come to us for the feast."

"No," Goda stamped her foot violently, "No! If you take me back I shall die."

It was a bright day. There was nowhere as beautiful as these soft Devon fields where, in spite of a film of ice over an oblong pond, a whole frozen world waited below the surface of earth and water to come to life with the first warm shower. The grass would begin to lift and the furze and the tiny worts show their green edges. There was no wind and Eldred threw back his hood. This was one of the walks that would come back into a man's mind when he was sitting after a good bargain over a pot of ale. He brushed aside a branch of trailing bramble, it was a bright winter red, and stopped in front of a little wood. Should he cross it or keep to the road? It would cut off half a mile but an old proverb flashed into his head, "The longest way round may prove the shortest in the end." There were fugitives about from the Wessex lands that the Duke had harried and he did not want to get a knife thrust into his back.

He wondered about the sword? He had seen it once, it was not an outstanding blade and he never forgot a weapon. Yet all arms were worth more now than during the previous years. He doubted that the Duke was ready to invade the West, he was too busy feasting after his conquests but it would come or King Harold's sons would try to rally the folk. The city had sent messengers to other towns to ask for men and the walls had been repaired during the summer. Under such conditions, the more arms a smith had to sell the better. Once there was fighting blades got broken, nicked or they simply disappeared and it took time, and fuel for the forge, to make an axe. Ulgar's son and his brother were surly and a bargain would be hard; he suspected he might have to leave without a purchase.

The path up to the farm when he got there was full of deep, slippery holes. It would be impossible to take a yoke of oxen along it. He thought he saw two eyes watching him from behind a blackberry bush and a tiny rustle as somebody slid away. The dead leaves smelled where the ditch had not been cleaned out and at one point part of the bank had fallen into a pit that smelled like a cesspool. Bad farming, he thought, and no order but he was not going to turn back now and he walked boldly up to the yard.

"What do you want?" a voice shouted angrily and then the man recognized him. "Good day, Master Eldred, have you come to look at the sword? Come in," he turned and shouted something to the barking dogs, "fortunately my brother is here, you can follow me freely, the hounds are tied."

Eldred picked his way across the untidy, stinking ground where a few slabs had been thrown down to give foothold above the mud. He did not like the appearance of the half-gnawed leashes tied to the animals that looked more like wolves but they recognized their master and sat sullenly on their haunches. "We are afraid of plunderers," the farmer said as if in explanation, "but we can give a good account of ourselves," and he nodded to a boy who stepped into the open with a bow and arrows, it was the urchin, no doubt, that Eldred had heard moving behind the hedge.

"Yes," the smith agreed, "times are bad."

"It's the carls of those young Godwins, they're worse than the Normans."

"They hanged a fellow the other day for robbing a barn."

"One man! And twenty go free."

He would be anxious if he lived on one of these isolated farms. The fugitives streaming to the West were men who had plowed their own fields. Their homes had been seized and their cattle driven away. It was natural, after they had wandered across half England and found neither shelter nor sympathy, that the taking of hens or even a sheep ceased to be a crime in their eyes. And he had heard tales as well of the reckless hunting of the Godwin youths. "Can I see the sword?" He expected he had come on a useless errand and was anxious to placate the men and leave.

The younger man did not speak while his brother fetched the blade nor did they offer him the customary wayfarer's ale. He could hear women talking in the back yard and another savage snarl from the dogs. The farmer slapped his burden down on a table that had not been washed for weeks and looked up hopefully at the smith.

"It has rusted." Eldred held the weapon up to the light.

"Oh, it's not deep, it's just the wet autumn we had, we're in a hollow here. A spot of grease and it will look like new."

Yet he would have to be honest about it to a purchaser, a man's life often depended upon how he was armed. Besides, rust tended to recur and the edge was so blunt that Eldred wondered if it had been used for cutting wood. "It would take me as much time and timber as forging a new one," he laid it down on the table again.

"Two silver shillings and it's yours."

Then there was certainly a flaw. A sword was worth more than two sheep and one of these was worth a shilling in the market. "Silver for this? I will give you three scythes."

"We have plenty of our own."

"I can understand you do not want to sell it. It belonged to your father. Take my advice, grease it, and hang it on the wall, that rust spreads like canker."

"A shilling then and two new spades." The man's face was impassive but he must want to make a sale, otherwise he would not continue bargaining.

"It's a bad year. I worked round Michaelmas for a fortnight on some bridle rings, then the merchant who had ordered them died, and his men could not pay for them."

"A shilling and two spades. It's our last offer."

Eldred lifted the sword again and felt the edge with his thumb. The more he looked at it the less he liked it. Yet he felt a growing uneasiness as the men waited for his reply. He had been a fool to come to so remote a place alone. "You are asking me for a gift but I accept," he tried to speak as heartily as if he were standing beside his own forge.

"You have the shilling?"

"What! Travel outside Exeter with silver?" He laughed as if they had been making a joke but his old training took command as if it had been yesterday and not eleven years since he had guarded the frontier. "Bring the sword to the market next week and the payment will be waiting for you." There was nothing to prove that they had intended to rob him had he been foolish enough to bring the price in his belt except their sullen uneasiness and his long experience of the border.

The farmer shouted and a woman brought in some watery ale and a plate full of scraps of stale bread. It was the custom to eat something after a bargain but he invited a man who brought him some tool to repair to his own board and gave him meat; it was a way to hear what was going on in the villages. He could hardly swallow the drink that they poured into a filthy mug and the younger brother said as if in self-defense, "The Godwins cleared out our barn a month ago."

"Yet I heard they paid for what they took?" They were stocking provisions inside the city.

"At the lowest price. Besides, they tempted our herdsman to join their band with talk of plunder. We need men to till fields, not swing axes."

"Yes," it was essential not to be provoked into an argument, "the times are bad. First the poor harvest two years ago, then the invasion and who knows what is in front of us next summer?"

"Let the Normans take us over if they want. I hear the farmers who submit to the Duke are protected and his officers pay well for what they need."

They heard. But from whom? Not from the fugitives, they had lost all they had. "What he does while he holds Wessex and what he might do if the West were his as well is a very different matter. But we have the winter, snow is not the time for a campaign." It was not true as he knew from Harold's winter war in Wales but he was getting as restive as a horse, he had to leave. "You will forgive me if I seem in a hurry," he got up taking care to keep the men in front of him, "but it's a long walk back to Exeter and they shut the gates so early."

He thought, to his surprise, that the men were as relieved as he was. "For your wife," the younger man took a cracked and tiny jar of honey from a shelf and pressed it into his hand and Eldred thanked him as if it were a royal gift. Perhaps they were simply frightened, overworked men and not thieves yet he could not reason away his acute suspicion that he was in danger. "I will take you as far as the gate on account of the dogs." The farmer opened the door and the stink of the muck in the never cleaned yard overpowered even the frosty air, "They are savage but we need them at night."

Life was like sword play, a succession of contrasts. Here was a sky the exact blue of the bellflowers growing up the ditches in spring, behind him was a yard of mud and wild hounds. Nobody knew if Harold's bones were really in that cairn beside the Narrow Seas, nor if the Duke was keeping the Christmas feast at Winchester. The past was the past, nothing would bring back moments that had once been fully experienced and even the gulls, although they might sweep across the river from Duryard moors to the open water, could not see the future.

Men could say what they liked, dream as they wished, but as certainly as the morning frost was on the blackthorn, the Duke's army would march into the West unless the Godwins set a trap for it further up the country. It was their only hope and yet whatever gold the Godwins had, it was not enough to hire the foreign soldiers they would need for such an enterprise. Few of the men here would follow them willingly; like the farmers that he had just left, their own bit of land was all that mattered to them. Besides, they had had no training. Was this the reason, he stopped so suddenly that his hood flew back and the cold bit his ears, that they had wanted to sell him the sword? An unarmed man was less likely to be summoned to the army and if the Duke should be triumphant, his officers would seize all weapons without payment. Must it always be the same, would the peasants never leave the fields till their flocks were driven away in front of them and all resistance was too late? Suddenly he was striding across the grass as if he were back with the housecarls again and the precarious peace that he had built up by refusing to remember, yes, refusing to remember, by saying before Stamford that he was a smith and that his rightful place was at the forge, swirled away like a drift of midsummer mist.

"Godric! Godric!" What did he mean, shouting the name aloud? He looked round uneasily but he was alone. He had never heard what had happened to the rest of his companions but a man had told a trader who had told a dealer in ponies who had once met him at a fair, that his old commander had had his wish. The Earl had finally given him a farm. And what had happened? He had died a month later in his bed. From black spotted fever or an ailment in his chest, the dealer was not certain which, but a cousin's son had inherited the place. Perhaps that was why the thane had looked so enviously at him when they parted. He had had some presentiment that time was flying off with his days (it was not only a few old women who could guess a person's fate) and had known each morning when he marched the band to their shield practice by the river that it was another whole day lost from his home.

And the others? Where were they? Too old, he supposed, to have fallen at Hastings. He thought of them rather as nursing their scars and agues around some village fire. He let, he encouraged, memories to flood over him that he had so sternly checked before, the great winter campaign following the Earl, the marches till they had driven "the hornets" from their own hills, a fire on a cliff, the summer raids. Hereford had had peace since that time.

Why be cautious? He would go back by the short cut and risk whatever surprises the wood held for him. His senses were alert, he was listening as in the old days to the little noises among the trees, bending a branch back here and there, treading on moss as soft as a woman's smock, no longer a sober Exeter citizen but a young housecarl insolently aware of what the bushes could hide till it did not surprise him when he heard a moan from the tangle on his right, it was exactly as if something had drawn him directly to the spot. A youth, without a cloak and with his head bent over his knees, groaned as he stopped in front of him.

"Get up! You'll freeze to death if you stay here."

The bundle did not stir and Eldred added, more gently, "Are you ill, fellow?"

The head lifted itself slowly. There were the unmistakable signs of starvation in the almost green face and, as the smith said later to his wife, "the bones were so sharp you could have used them for a whetstone."

"The sooner I die, the sooner it's over." The exertion of speaking seemed so great that the figure slumped forward even further, it was a scarecrow with dangling arms rather than a man.

"Are you from Wessex?" As a smith and citizen of his native city, Eldred had turned plenty of fugitives away. They brought in diseases and ate up the reserves. Yet now, with his border memories ranging brightly through his mind, he saw the fellow as a victim of some sudden foray and he could not leave him.

"I am Edgar, son of Edmund. My father was a thane and was killed among the bodyguard. The Normans seized our farm."

Whatever he wished, the smith could not carry the apparently dying youth as far as the city. If he went there for help it would be almost nightfall and time to close the gates. He looked down at the figure, the worn jerkin had once been good leather but the rags that Edgar had wrapped around his legs were filthy and torn. What would Elfleda say? Elfleda! The basket she wanted. He had forgotten all about it till this moment but old Alfhelm could not be more than a quarter of a mile away. He forced himself to grab the putrid tatters that were doubly horrible in the crisp, clean air. "Get up, try to walk, I may be able to find you shelter in a barn not far from here."

"You're a God-fearing man, I know," Alfhelm's face was exactly like the round muzzle of a friendly dog, "but what we give these fugitives comes out of our children's mouths and our own stores."

There was a pile of rushes yellowing to white beside the hut, a half made basket stood on a flat stone, everything was in its usual place and Eldred wondered what had happened to upset the old man? They had been friends ever since Alfhelm had shown him a magnificent crab apple tree inside the woods and he had given him a curved and specially sharpened knife to cut his reeds. "Keep Edgar till he can walk and I will bring you some meal."

"You are a busy man and will forget."

"Look, I will leave my brooch as pledge," the smith unfastened the clasp, he had made it himself in the rough shape of a dragon and was proud of it.

"You cannot give to every beggar you see."

"His father died with the bodyguard and I fought under the King, he was an Earl in those days, in Wales."

"Let him die. It's kinder, he has no land and no craft."

Perhaps the youth thought the same. He had uttered no word of gratitude but had shuffled along with Eldred's good arm round him, as if unwilling to break his death sleep. "Give him shelter," he pressed his brooch into the old man's hand, "I will fetch him, I swear, before Christmas."

It still seemed as if his efforts were in vain but some

footsteps came shuffling down the path. Hearing the voices, the old man's wife had left her spinning wheel and come to join them. "Another one?" She looked at Edgar who had slid onto the grass again. "It's not the crust I grudge them but one stole a basket that was drying here in the sun and we're afraid they will murder us. We pile stones against the door every night."

"Yes!" There was an expression of angry terror in Alfhelm's eyes that Eldred had never noticed before. "You have the walls at Exeter but what should we do if they set the hut on fire?" He looked back at his two bee-hives behind the wattle fence, at another pile of reeds and the strip of ground dug up for the spring planting. "Still, help me to get him to the barn and he can stay but no longer than four days."

"And I will get an old sheepskin to put over him, he needs warmth first more than food."

III

It was seldom that the ice formed on the river but the flat, gray water flowed so evenly between the banks that it might have been the tongue of a frozen lake. The landscape lacked the magnificence of the Kentish cliffs or the thick forests behind the Irish coast but whether it was its peacefulness or because the wet green of the meadows stirred a memory of his father's country that he had left before he was barely old enough to walk, this was the place that he would always think of as home. Yet he was a foreigner, a man whom even his friend Eldred called "the Frisian" instead of addressing him as Thorkell, "a name common all over the North," as his father had explained when asked why he had not been called after his grandfather as was the usual custom; all but born here but unable to become a citizen. The sea was his real country but a sailor needed somewhere to think about when the spray stung his eyes, a spot to which he could return in winter or old age, and dream about when he was in danger. The path that he was following had been trodden bare by the fishermen and he could already see his ship. It was moored in the Exe among a dozen others, the deck covered with straw and canvas to keep out the wet, but come April when the winds began to lift the grass, gently and not tearing at it as now, the *Seabird* would come to life again, ready for a new journey.

A gull rose into the air and another screeched. The sound brought·back thoughts that he preferred to ignore. So had such birds risen above the landing at Pevensey, so had they wheeled about the burial cairn on the cliff. They had wings, they could circle above the conquerors but what had the Sussex peasants been able to do but die?

"Why, Eldred!" He wondered what his friend was doing beside the river on a market morning, "That's not one of your blades." Thorkell pulled the cloak round him that a sudden gust of wind had blown back from his arms, it was going to be a very cold day.

"No, it belonged to Ulgar's father. He did not want to keep it so I went over and saw it at his farm. A waste of time perhaps because there is not much that I can do with it but I enjoyed the walk. We agreed a price and he brought it to me today."

"Better keep it till the summer. You'll get more for it when the rumors start again."

"They say the Duke is keeping Christmas at Winchelsea. It's too near the West for my liking."

"I suppose we are safe till spring." The wind had got

under a flap of canvas, Thorkell noted, he must send one of his men down with another rope.

"I wonder what the young Godwins are thinking? Now would be the time to make a raid."

"The young Godwins are thinking about their hawks."

Yet the moment to attack was when the army had stacked its weapons and begun to drink. Harold's leadership might have saved them but his sons were inexperienced and too young. "Why are you looking at the *Seabird*? Is an awning loose? I suppose you are planning to sail as early as possible in the spring?"

What a strange thing birth was! As if a baby were even conscious of it! So even his friend was suggesting that he did not belong here and would abandon Exeter if the city were in danger. Perhaps he would, Thorkell dug the toe of his heavy shoe angrily into the ground, but not because he was afraid to stand beside them on the walls but because if there were a truce, they might choose him as a hostage, the more powerful among the citizens used him but did not like him, and he had sailed too far and too often to face a half captivity for years in a dingy keep. "How should I know, Eldred? The winds will decide."

They turned together and started slowly towards the city, their thoughts, if it had been a moment to exchange them, as dreary as the weather. "I found a youth in the woods the other day," what had his friend got on his mind? His face was set in the grim lines of a man marching into battle. "A thane's son, whose father was killed beside the standard."

"A long wandering if he really came from Sussex."

"He has their speech, we had a Sussex man with us in the housecarls and at first we couldn't understand him."

"But you've got your man, Merewin, and the boy for the forge."

"It's my duty to save an orphan if his father died at Hastings but I shall never understand women. Elfleda for some reason refuses to let me bring him to the house."

Elfleda spread the cloak in front of her as if the rip at the shoulder was all that mattered in the world. She was glad actually to have something over which she could bend so as to keep the triumph out of her eyes. After a terrible scene with Goda, she had left the girl shrieking on the stone floor of Queen Gytha's hall and now, instead of a long and possibly unsuccessful fight with Eldred over her daughter, if she were careful, the situation was in her hands.

"He can sleep in the shed by the forge." It was no place for a thane's son, still the smith dared not propose that Edgar should come into the house.

"But he eats, I suppose?"

"I have told you, Elfleda, I will get you another sack of meal."

"You have just come from the market, have you heard what the farmers are asking merely for a bag?"

"His father died with the housecarls."

"Then take him to the Godwins."

"I shall in the spring." At present they were turning

many of their retainers away, they could not find food for them. "It is just for the winter months until he can wield an axe." What was the matter with Elfleda? He had often reproached her for giving too large a lump of bread to some urchin who had simply carried up a bundle from the market but she seemed to have taken a dislike to Edgar before even seeing him. "He is without friends here and so young."

"They knew in Sussex there would be an invasion."

"And they know here that the Duke may march on Exeter."

It was out! Everybody expected it but, to save her, she supposed from anxiety, Eldred up to now had always found some argument against it. Now he had had to admit the possibility. She wondered briefly why he was so afraid of trusting her? It was like this cloak, he could find a dozen reasons why it was torn but would never agree that it was because he snatched his brooch open in a hurry instead of gently undoing the clasp. "I've saved wood and weighed meal all summer to please you and now you want to add a sick man to the household."

"It's the first time I've ever known you refuse to help the unfortunate."

"Why should I care for yet another fugitive when my own daughter is sick with misery inside that gloomy hall? What is the use of what you call a courtly training to Goda? She is not even likely to marry a thane, and what has she learned except to be unhappy since she left my care?" All that mattered was to get Goda home again but she drew the two edges of the cloth together as if matching the stitches were of prime importance and with immense control, she did not look up at her husband's face.

"An exchange, I see." He had spent a year's savings on bribing various officials in order to place his stepdaughter in the Queen's household and now, he saw, it had been wasted. "Couldn't she wait at least till Easter?" The girl disliked her stepfather and found a number of trifling but irritating ways to annoy him.

"If anything happens, if the Duke besieges Exeter, my daughter's place is here. It is only what any mother would ask."

That of course was different. It was an aspect of the matter that he had forgotten and not, as he had thought, a peevish girl tyrannizing her mother to get her own way but a reasonable request. "Very well, if the Queen is willing you may bring her home but see that she is silent at table and keeps her hair well covered in the street. Oh, and put a fleece or two in the outhouse. I want to fetch Edgar today while there are people about on the roads." There were too many fugitives banding together to kill a man for a cloak or the food he might have on him, to risk being on the woodland paths at dusk.

The wind had dropped. Alfhelm was sitting on a bench outside his hut with the frame of a new basket balanced on a stool in front of him and some reeds piled loosely at his side. Eldred suspected that he had been waiting for him for hours. "It's exactly the fourth day," he pushed enough rushes away to be able to sit down next the old man.

"The boy can walk," Alfhelm twisted a particularly tough stem between his fingers and then tossed it impatiently to the ground, "but what's the use? There's no work for him at Exeter." He hated foreigners and foreigners included even men from the neighboring villages.

"The Godwins will take him in the spring and till then he can help my forge boy with the fires."

"You're lucky to have enough to feed him." He forced another reed so stubbornly through the frame that one of the stakes bent. "There was too little sun last summer to dry the rushes properly," he grumbled as he tried to straighten it out.

"Where is the boy? I have brought him some old clothes."

"Edgar? When I saw him last he was sweeping the yard. Edgar!" The old voice was too weak to carry far if the youth had not been waiting to be summoned. He came from behind a stack of wood in his leather coat and some leggings that they had lent him; they bunched at the knees and barely came down to the middle of his legs.

"Here you are!" Eldred tossed him the bundle, "Make haste, they shut the gates now before it is dark."

"I'll be ready in a moment," Edgar whispered as if he had almost lost his voice as well but then he added as an afterthought, like a child given a cake, "thank you for bringing them."

"If anything happens, Alfhelm," the little hut that was the shape and color of a beehive seemed so unprotected in these woods, "come to me at once. There will always be a place with us for your wife and yourself."

"Happen! What is likely to happen before the spring? Do you think an army can march along a frozen road?"

Yet that was how the Earl had beaten the Welsh, eleven, twelve, no, now it was thirteen years ago and even if Godric's troop had been assigned to the rearguard, he had been with the army. He still remembered the bite of the cold from the ground and how men had fought each other for places next the fire at night. It was more likely that the Duke would come in April or as they began to cut the hay in June but the first thing that a housecarl learned was to watch and not to imagine. "You should have come to the market this morning and seen the walls. They have been repairing them all summer."

"It's enough if I have to come at Michaelmas. I don't like being jostled by strangers nor having dogs knock over all my wares. Besides, why should the Normans come here? They've got all Sussex. But then," he looked up with a malicious grin, "you're rich in Exeter. You have to find something to do with your pennies."

"Oh, we pay dues for permission to breathe." He had not liked giving up a month's earnings towards paying for the laborers although he had known that the work was necessary. "I've brought you some meal for looking after Edgar," he put a small bag on the seat, "and what about a basket for Elfleda? I've a knife you could have for it."

"This will see us through the winter!" He had not noticed Alfhelm's wife join them but she picked up the bag and hugged it as if it were a child. Was it age or had her many wrinkles come from always living in the open air? Both she and her husband had skins the color of a long dried drop of honey.

"A basket? What about this?" Alfhelm leaned over to pick one out from a row standing near him.

"If you had one a little bigger . . ." the knife that he was offering was small but very sharp.

"She needs a basket for her washing, Alfhelm, not for market," the old woman interrupted, "I'll get the big one from the hook in the shed."

The trees were near enough to shelter the hut but not so close as to keep out the sunshine. There were bushes and herbs growing in a small patch of garden and two hives of bees. Eldred did not want to frighten the old people but he had to explain to them how conditions had changed. "Move into the next village for the winter or come to us. There are strangers about and some of them are armed."

"The dog will warn us and we bar the door at night."

"It's the men the Normans have driven out of their farms."

"We're too far away and I'm not going to leave my home."

Eldred had once seen the ears of a young hare brush against a clump of grass and startle, in so doing, a fawn on its way to the water. He could not warn the beasts that a hunt was planned for that very spot the following day but only leave them to the satisfactions of the moment. It was the same with the old couple, force them to come to Exeter and they would probably die. Possibly there was some safety in the forest that had become by now a part of them?

"Will this do?" The basket that Alfhelm's wife put down in front of him was certainly one that she had intended to use herself.

"It's exactly what Elfleda needs." Perhaps now she would forgive him for whatever it was that had angered her. He offered Alfhelm the knife and watched him feel the edge and balance the weight of it on his palm. He did not speak but the smith was used to these sudden silences, he often wondered if the couple exchanged a dozen words during the course of the day, but it was late and he wanted to leave. Yet where was his brooch? He did not want to lose it, partly because Elfleda would reproach him and partly because it was one that he had made for himself. "And the token? It's time we started home."

"The token?" Alfhelm scratched his ear as if it were the first time that he had heard of it. "The token? Oh, yes, your brooch. Now what did I do with it?" He stepped over the reeds so as not to disturb them and shuffled into the house.

"It's dark inside," his wife said as if in explanation, "I let the fire smolder till it gets dark."

Eldred yawned. It was the cold but he felt that he was lying in the open again, not quite awake but aware that there was nobody beside him to throw more peat onto the embers. "I have left the leggings beside the fleeces," Edgar's voice tugged him back to his senses, "and I hung the cup on the hook." The youth had put on the clothes that the smith had brought him but he still had his leather coat over his arm. "It's clean," Alfhelm's wife noticed that Eldred was looking at it, "I beat the fleas out myself with a bunch of gorse."

"There's nothing like gorse for driving fleas away." Eldred was about to tell the boy to leave the jacket all the same when he remembered how he had clung to the remnants of his housecarl days long after he had reached Exeter: a twig that he had whittled into the shape of an arrowhead to show Godric that he could still hold a piece of wood in his left hand and an old belt that had split at the clasp. "We must start," he stared into the hut but it was so dark that all he could see was a moving shape like a shadow, "it will take two hours to reach the gate."

They stood there not knowing what to say until, minutes later, Alfhelm came out with the brooch. "Here it is," he flicked a feathery bit of green away with his finger, "I wrapped it up in moss."

"My thanks for looking after the boy," to his surprise, Edgar bent over the old woman and kissed her as if she had been his mother, "and whenever you wish, come to us at Exeter."

"Houses make cowards," Alfhelm's nose wrinkled with delight at his joke, "if the army comes this way, I know two hollow trees that will be a better shelter than your walls. But the frost is master even of the Duke. Go and watch your fire until it is time to plow and then come and see me, I'll give you a bunch of the first gorse buds then for your wife. If she steeps them well in ale they will drive away your winter coughs in a week."

IV

"Warm at New Year, wet at harvest," Osmund quoted and Eldred, glancing down the table, thought the steersman with his round head and short gray beard was exactly like a seal, although the only time he had seen such a beast was when a dead one had been washed up on the shore. "It may be mild for January but after the dinner you have offered us, it would not hurt to fast for a month," and the smith bowed to the Frisian, while washing his fingers in a bowl a servant offered to him.

"We cannot match Dame Elfleda's Christmas feast. I woke up last night and thought of the beef she served us."

"She is a good cook but I cannot remember when I have eaten as well as I have today." Eldred glanced up at the gay hunting scene embroidered on a curtain hanging opposite him on the wall. These merchants were richer than a smith could hope to be but he did not grudge his friend his wealth; every summer some ships were lost.

"They say the Duke kept Christmas at Winchester," Osmund growled, he was so used to shouting orders that his voice sounded as gruff as a challenge.

"Oh, don't spoil the day by mentioning him," Thorkell interrupted, it was a dangerous subject partly because he could see the youth Eldred had rescued who was the fourth at the table, biting his lips to keep from comment and also because it was wiser for a trader to be silent. Sooner or later the Normans would come to Exeter. He felt it in his bones much as he felt the first stirring of a storm. The townspeople repeated that the Duke's losses had been heavy, his soldiers wanted to enjoy the farms they had seized, there were even rumors all was not well in his own Duchy and there was no reason for him to march against the independent West. They believed their isolation would protect them. Thorkell, with five voyages behind him, knew that it added to their danger. They ought to post the most skillful of their men along the borders to bring them news of any suspicious move, they should try to gain allies, even among their hated foes, the Welsh, they should improve their defenses and gain time. As it was, the elders comforted themselves with every stray rumor that confirmed what they wanted to hear but was so rarely based on fact. Conquest only made a man hungry to continue war. Did he not plan himself another voyage directly the *Seabird* had dropped anchor in the Exe? He had invited his guests solely (did Eldred know it?) to hear first hand what Edgar could tell him about the nine months he had spent under Norman rule and what he had found on his journey to the city.

"We're safe for another year," Eldred moved a little so that they could remove the last dishes from the table, "but I'm not as certain as some are that there won't be trouble in time. I think a lot of people are uneasy, I've had more old weapons brought me during the last weeks to sharpen or mend than I had formerly in twelve months."

"Winter is the time for stories," Thorkell refilled the drinking cups himself, "if Master Eldred does not mind hearing it again, tell us how you reached Exeter?" The firelight caught Edgar's face, it was flushed with anger, not with ale.

"I was a boy when the summons came for my father to join the King. Our estate was not as large as those of our neighbors but the land was rich and we had much timber. He took four men with him and I begged to go as well but I had not come to my full strength."

"You need to be seventeen before you can swing an axe properly." Oh, the impatient waiting of his youth! Eldred's shoulders twitched, he thought of the hours he had stood in the yard where he still worked, wanting the days to pass that stretched always more drearily from dawn to twilight and knowing he could not seek his independence till he was full grown. Yet he must have come to manhood earlier than this thane's son, because of his heavy work at the forge.

"I walked with them as far as the stream although I had to run while they strode. My father patted my shoulder when we came to the stepping stones and told me to look after the farm." The water had been full of dead leaves and the oxherd, standing beside his father, had raked out a bent reed with his hook. "I went home slowly, it was the first time I was really afraid but something inside me knew that I should never see my father again." The familiar figure was clear in memory, showing him how to ride or hold a falcon on his wrist, only the last picture was indistinct, five black dots disappearing into the distance between the trees.

"That can happen," Thorkell said gravely and they all nodded.

"Without grief how should we know what is joy?" Osmund quoted and the smith wondered if people ever thought about the meaning of the words when they heard them in a stave?

"We waited. It was time to turn the pigs out into the woods and I helped our swineherd to watch them. Usually I was happy in the forest but that October if my belt strap caught in a bush or a piglet got lost, I felt it was an omen against us and I could not laugh as I would have done the previous year. I ought to have kept a tally stick but again something prevented me and I don't know how many days it was when one evening, we were just fastening the gates for the night, I saw Sigeric approaching. I did not know it was Sigeric at first, his clothes were tattered and there was that green look on his face that comes from hunger, but then he called me."

"And you knew?"

"I knew."

"Were they with the bodyguard?" Eldred's own

place would have been two places beyond Godric in the line.

"No, they were too lightly armed. Only my father had a coat of mail. They were posted with the levies to the left of the housecarls in the middle of the marshes. It was when they were rushing down to finish off some Normans caught in the bog that an arrow caught my father in the throat."

"Arrows! A man's weapon is the axe." The smith almost rose from his stool and Thorkell put out a hand to restrain him.

"The second oxherd was killed as well and a third man wounded. It grew dark and there were soldiers wandering about the fields. They carried my father's body to a clearing and buried him there because the Normans had burned the neighboring villages on their march. They brought my father's sword and the oxherd's hook back with them but the wounded man had to stop at a farm and he did not get back to us till spring."

"Was it long before the Normans reached you?"

"Long?" Edgar gulped the ale in his cup as if he were still being pursued. "Only a few days. My uncle was the oldest man in the village and he was living at our hall. He sent me off to the woods because some said the soldiers were killing every man they could find. The Norman losses had been very heavy and they wanted to avenge them. I did not want to go but he said my mother would die if they stabbed me in front of her eyes and he thought we should form a new army, and I could join it, as men got back from the North."

"He was right." Eldred nodded approvingly, Godric

had always trained them not to run needlessly into danger.

"The battle came too soon after Stamford," Thorkell threw another log onto the fire, "that was the axe fight, Eldred, you prefer and there were few survivors." He hated the Normans as much as the smith but changes were inevitable. There was a moment of the swing when the best housecarl left his body exposed whereas an archer could pick a man off some distance away and never be himself in danger.

"I was in the forest when they actually came. Our swineherd was a man like Alfhelm and I doubt if one of our own villagers would have found us. Any other year I should have enjoyed it although it was already getting cold." He had rounded up the pigs that were not his pigs any longer and crouched in misery over a tiny blaze, always looking over his shoulder, always feeling as hunted as any miserable hare, because a foreign Duke who had been a shadowy name to most of them, had seized and devastated the land.

"And your village?" Thorkell's uneasiness increased with every word and he felt that he must drain the last drop of news from the unhappy youth in front of him. Every time the anchor was hauled up, the sailor faced a battle but the sea taught him to be flexible. The old ways were over now, only those able to change would survive.

"They did not trouble my uncle because of his age but they took our hall and forced my mother and her maids to cook for them and sleep together in one small room at the back of the dairy. They stole our winter supplies, killed all the cattle they could find, then they left two men on guard and marched away. One man struck them when they took his cow and they strung him up on a tree."

"How did the winter pass?"

"The swineherd had a hut so deep in the woods that no Norman was likely to find it. Once or twice when it seemed safe, I slipped back to the orchard to see my mother but she was so frightened of the guards' finding me, I never stayed with her long. Then in the black season after the New Year they got the winter fever badly in the village and she died. What had she to live for? They had killed my father, taken her home, and I was living, almost like an animal, in the forest."

"There was no hope," they all muttered round the fire and remembering the starving figure he had found among the leaves, the smith knew that Edgar would prefer their acceptance of the facts to sympathy.

"I wanted to get away but what could I do? There were rumors that those who submitted would be allowed to keep a little of their land and my uncle urged me to wait, he thought one day I could return to the village. Yet others grumbled, this wasn't mended or the well was half dry, but this was due to their own carelessness, not my father. Besides, there were places that I never wanted to see again, the stepping stones and the room where my mother had died without my being with her."

"I should have felt the same." Thorkell did not want to stir up memories that were better forgotten but how had the youth contrived to get to Exeter? It had once taken him ten days to sail half the distance in the *Sea-bird*.

"The months went on till it was past midsummer. Sometimes I was resentful, there I was, living like an outlaw, on my own land. Then there were moments when the air itself seemed silver and free."

"I know," Thorkell agreed, "some days sing."

"I heard voices when I came back to the hut one evening and I should have crept away only I recognized Egbert's voice. He farmed a piece of land for one of our neighbors and we had heard the Normans had taken his cattle. 'So you want to go beyond the seas as well,' he said without any other greeting when I joined them and I thought I had never seen such anger in any man's face."

They sat in as deep a silence for a moment as the exiles must have known that night. One day they had been prosperous citizens, even a bondman had his couple of sheep; the next, the rights and meadows that had come to them from their ancestors were in the hands of strangers, speaking a foreign language. "So you decided to follow Egbert," Thorkell asked, filling up the cups another time.

"The swineherd just said he would tell my uncle and I felt that even he was glad to see me go. I had no preparations to make because I had already taken my clothes and my father's sword to the hut to save them from the Normans. I was so thankful to be on my way at last that it was only when we climbed a hill the following day and Egbert said, 'Say farewell to your valley, you'll never see it again,' that I realized how uncertain a future I had chosen. I suppose I looked startled because Egbert laughed at me, 'It's gone, boy, it's gone, forget about it.' Yet how could I put my birthplace and the sixteen years I had lived in it, out of my mind in a single moment?" Edgar looked gratefully across the table at Eldred, he was still amazed that a man as respected as the smith should have troubled to drag him to safety.

"Our Council might be stouter hearted if they realized what conquest brings with it. But go on, tell us more about your journey."

"Egbert had arranged to join a band, eventually there were five of us, there were too many outlaws about to travel alone. Those first few days were like a holiday. The berries on the brambles were still tight green knots and I could smell the second crop of yellow blossoms on the furze. Then one morning we climbed up a height and I saw a gray, moving field below us . . ."

"And you did not need Egbert to tell you it was the sea."

"I felt if I were on a ship, I should not have to drop on hands and knees among the prickles every time we heard a voice. We should be safe."

"It would depend on whether it were stormy or not," the Frisian had vivid memories of running before the wind along the coast. Yet he could understand Edgar's feelings. They were like the audacity of the gulls. These rose and dived at will, it seemed nothing could harm them, yet he had often found a dead one on the beach.

"I had no cares. Egbert was like a second father to

me and it was he who decided on Exeter. 'They speak our language and it will be easier to get there than Flanders.' We started as soon as it was light, slept a little at midday and then walked on again till it was too dark to see. Mostly we kept close to the cliffs, there was usually a patch that the sheep had bitten bare and the shepherds were kind to us. It was the end of the tenth day when we lost the trace of a path and had to force our way through some bushes. They were low and beaten down by the wind. I remember looking up at an evil, green sky and wondering if we were walking directly into a storm? We were tired and perhaps not as careful as usual. I heard a sudden yell and saw Egbert fall. I thought he had caught his foot in a root but then the adder slithered past me, it was the dangerous time, they all come out at dusk."

"Any child knows that! It bit him, I suppose, we had a lot of trouble with snakes in Wales." The first thing that they had done when they had made a camp, was to poke round all the bushes with a stick.

"In the middle of his leg." Edgar would never forget that flat yellow head disappearing into the grass nor his friend's harsh scream.

"Did he die?"

"I do not think so. The yell brought a shepherd to us and he had a root with him they keep for such bites. They lose a lot of lambs from the adders every spring. He cut round the wound and Egbert kept vomiting, he said that was a good sign. We carried him between us to the shepherd's hut and his wife gave him a syrup made from a bramble I did not know and poulticed the wound with mugwort. He was still alive the next morning and ordered me to go on with the others, there was not enough food for us to stay. I gave my little knife to the woman who said she would look after him and how I missed it later! It's hard to cut one's meat with a dagger."

For a time nobody spoke and Edgar stared at the fire as if he could see the remaining stages of his voyage in its embers. What had happened to his friend? He often wondered guiltily if he ought to have risked starvation and stayed with him? "I wish I knew if Egbert got to the coast. I waited almost a week for him but he never came."

"The poison spreads through the whole body. It might have been days before he could walk."

"It took us longer than we expected to reach the shore. The adder had frightened us all and we went round bushes instead of through them. Finally we came to the harbor. . . ."

"And couldn't even find a coracle!" Thorkell had often wondered why they made so little use of several excellent ports.

"There was one boat but that was when I missed Egbert so much. I had had no experience of bargaining and I had to give the captain my best cloak in exchange for a passage. The others with me decided to wait till spring but Egbert's words were running through my head, 'The Norman influence is spreading like a tide and by next April it will be too late to reach the West.' It was the end of September and I remember thinking it was almost a year since the invasion. I longed for my home as we pulled out from the wharf but I knew I should never see it again. How happy I had been there as a boy and how little I had known this."

"We are heedless if fortune is with us and what we remember is a shadow." Thorkell laid a stick carefully on the fire, there was his own boyhood expedition along the Exe, a strange, windy morning that he had wanted to hold in his hands till in pure excitement, if a sailor had not shouted at him, he would have steered his skiff straight to the open sea.

"The ship began to toss and I could think of nothing then but my own misery. We rolled sideways, I shrieked, all the seamen laughed but I really thought we were turning upside down. The boat righted itself and I began to breathe again but a few moments afterwards I was so ill that I hoped we should sink."

"It's soon over, the ship sickness, and it rarely comes again."

"Not so soon, or it wasn't with me. The worst of my journey was to come and I think this was partly due to my head being so muddled when I landed. I heard of a group of fugitives going on to Exeter but again I had to give the leader most of the possessions I still owned before he would let me join them. The country was difficult, we were always losing our way and my companions kept quarreling and fighting with one another. The farmers did not mind giving a man a bowl of milk or a bit of cheese in summer but it was drawing near to the leanest time of the year. One night there was a storm and when the wind dropped, I was sleepy but I woke up in the morning to find myself alone. My sword, the only thing that was left me, had gone."

"Only an outlaw would rob a comrade in misfortune," the smith snapped a twig in two and flung it into the flames as if he wished that it had been one of the band, "who were those men? It was leaving you to a slow death."

"They had all lost their homes or their land," Edgar preferred not to think about waking that morning, "fortunately the first person I met was a swineherd and once he saw that I knew something about pigs, he took me into his hut. I meant to stay with him during the winter but he came back from the village one day with a rumor that the Duke had not disbanded his army and was planning a march. I was a fool, I know now, but I started on my journey again, they said I was about a week away from here, but I lost my way and when you found me," he looked gratefully up at Eldred, "I was almost dead."

How much the boy had faced because of his loyalty! The smith leaned forward and patted Edgar on the shoulder. "You'll make a good housecarl once we put some flesh on your bones. Stay with us till March and I'll ask Redwald to take you into the Godwin following."

"You were lucky," the steersman added, "many youths must have quitted their homes as you did and perished on the way here."

"I blame the man who stole your weapon, you might easily have died."

"Loss breeds lawlessness," Thorkell filled the bowls a final time from a now almost empty jug, "but for once, the tale had a good ending. If Redwald cannot take you in the spring, come to me."

1068

V

They're too late."

"Why don't they hurry?"

"They can't move faster than their sheep can walk."

Was it worth while waiting, Eldred wondered, among these idle onlookers for another wretched group of fugitives to enter Exeter? A wall had risen once the Duke's march was known, not between the guards and the approaching invaders, but between citizen and citizen. Eldred knew a single law, that he owed his loyalty to his overlords, the Godwins, and from what he heard among the passers-by, the folk felt the same although many had lost their farms; it was the Council and the elder thanes who had hurriedly sent messengers to the Normans, asking for terms.

"We should be better off in our homes," he turned, hearing a familiar voice, to find the Frisian standing at his elbow, "but I'm too restless to stay in mine. I suppose you have heard nothing new?"

"I saw my wife's cousin this morning" (he was careful to conceal these feelings from Elfleda but was there any man he disliked more than Frain?), "he thought the Council was right to submit."

"A little gain for much loss. It's a bad bargain."

"We have the walls and the defenders," Eldred spoke a little louder than he needed but there was a murmur of agreement round him, "all the Council lacks is the will to resist."

"Ready!" The officer in charge of the gate nodded to the waiting soldiers.

"Oh, give them a moment more, they're almost here." The fugitives were within bowshot, they were driving a flock of sheep in front of them and a man in a green hood and a patched jerkin was leading two ponies with shaggy, winter coats, behind them.

"I have my orders." Yet his men seemed to linger deliberately with their fingers on the bars.

"But they're our own folk," somebody shouted from the edge of the crowd, "and there isn't a Norman in sight." A boy left the group and began to run forward, holding an old brown cloak back with one hand. "Wait! Wait a moment more . . ." but the gate would have been shut, leaving the villagers between the invading army and the city if Thorkell had not cried out, "Look! A horseman! He must be bringing back a message."

"It's thane Eadnoth's man, I recognize the horse," a

citizen managed to push his way between the officer and the guard.

"They say the Godwins have barricaded themselves into their houses and mean to fight," Thorkell whispered so that only the smith could hear him, "but what about the Queen?"

"She'll take sanctuary." There was an outburst of talk among the crowd and all eyes were fixed upon the approaching messenger. He might hold their lives in his hand and each man hoped to see a hint of what might happen to him in the rider's face as he galloped past.

"A little wider," the officer pointed to the gate.

The horseman held up a token, he did not speak and it would have needed a wiser man even than the Frisian to guess from the impassive features the success or failure of his errand. The sheep began to flood in at his heels, bleating, scratching at a clump of wayside grass and an old man muttered, shifting the rushes that he carried on his shoulder, "At least we shall have extra food." He prodded a beast with his dirty fingers.

"Master Eldred!" An elderly woman came towards him with a basket hung over one arm and another, narrower one slung on her back, but for a moment the smith, whose thoughts were in the Council Hall, did not recognize her. Then he remembered the clearing in the forest. "I'm thankful you are here but where is Alfhelm? Have you left him behind?"

"He's dead." She spoke as calmly as if she were explaining why they had not fulfilled some order. "Three nights ago it was bitterly cold and I asked him to put another log on the fire. When he did not move, I got up and went to him but he must have died in his sleep. He had not been well for some days but he would have it that it was only the weather. I went to my kinsfolk to get help and found them packing up to move. I believe Alfhelm heard the Normans coming although they were miles away from us. He said he would never leave our hut."

"I warned him the last time I saw him."

"The woods were his lair, he was nearer to the trees, I used to tell him, than to men."

"You will be most welcome to our house," even Elfleda would not object to an old, helpless woman taking shelter in their kitchen.

"Thank you," she shook her head, "but I am glad to be with my kinsfolk again. I am grateful to have left that hut. I used to wake in terror, thinking I heard footsteps walking round the clearing. Alfhelm said they would never find us but with so many outlaws, how could he know? There were little slithering noises at the coldest time of the night and I never knew if they were mice or leaves or shoes. But how is Edgar? Has the boy recovered?"

"You will hardly recognize him. I will send him over to fetch you tomorrow because my wife will want to see you. But where are you going and what is your kinsman's name?"

"We are staying with Wulfric the carpenter. His house is in the second street from the Quay Gate."

"A good man, I know him," Thorkell interrupted, "last year he made me three new oars."

"He always gave us a feast when we came to the fair at Michaelmas," she smiled at the memory, it had been the great event of her year. Somebody called and she looked round anxiously, "I must go, I must go, I'm afraid of getting lost." She hurried off to join four people who were waiting for her with her dog barking at her heels.

"They are sending a deputation to the Duke," the man running towards them shouted out the news as soon as he could be heard, "they are offering the tribute we have always paid."

"The Normans are greedy, they'll ask more."

"They have taken hostages with them."

"Shame!" The crowd was getting angry, "He is not our overlord."

"Disperse! Leave the way to the gate free. Disperse!" Eldred nodded to Thorkell and as the guard began to push the people aside, they walked rapidly up the street.

It was unwise to talk aloud among the throngs round the gates and yet Eldred was too restless to sit inside his house. The factions seemed equally divided between those who cried the Duke was not their overlord and others who did not want their meadows turned into battlefields. It was a hard choice for many citizens although not for himself; without loyalty he could see no meaning in life. He took up the sword that he had bought from Ulgar's sons and began to polish it. Merewin, his forge man, had done his job well, it was thin but free from rust and sharpened to a good edge. Yet if they surrendered as it seemed they would, who would need a weapon? He envied the Frisian who could put to sea in May, if only he could join him! A vain wish, he could not leave Elfleda and the forge. Ah, the forge! It had hung round his neck like a burden, first as a boy when he was serving his father and afterwards when no leech could straighten his elbow and he had known that his dream of returning to Godric, swinging an axe from hand to hand, was simply —a dream. He walked up and down the yard, looking at the neat pile of logs, the rougher heap of small twigs, the broken tools waiting to be mended and asked himself what this narrow, tidy space had to do with being alive? Frain would be happy, he supposed Elfleda was there now, chattering to his wife Mildburh, her great friend, about how amazing it was that a victor should show such clemency and how, after all, they could go out and dig their simples up in spring. What would he say if the Normans started swaggering through the market place or people muttered, "What did the Godwins do but drink and hunt?" They ought to have marched against Winchester but after all, what were they but boys? And then a nagging thought came into his head, had he been other than a youth when he had followed Godric across the border, with sweat pouring down his face from under the leather cap that they were never allowed to remove? Godric had been older, had held them back like a leash of young hounds or loosed them to rush forward, usually against a foe that vanished into the bushes like a hare. Yes, the citizens here had never slept outside their homes nor broken the curfew to court a girl in the shelter of bracken and twigs, a girl who could not speak their language and who (as they were warned but who heeded the warning?) might cut their throats once they were asleep. How different, how different, from Elfleda whose feelings existed as thoughts. Exeter was old; it worshiped security and the irritating proverb of its citizens, "It all happens for the best."

What should he do with this sword? Hang it on the wall as a relic of an earlier day or sell it, for a good price, to one of the Frisian's sailors? If they actually put a garrison in the town he would leave, whether his wife liked it or not, before they put chains on his wrists.

"Master Eldred!" Edgar burst into the yard, breathless and without a cap, "Come to the walls, we're free."

"Free? What do you mean? What are the surrender terms? Are they marching into Exeter?"

"The thanes came back and declared the Duke's terms. He would not increase the tribute but we were all to acknowledge him as overlord and the Godwins must leave. In return, he would not molest the city. But the citizens rose, they shut the Council into its own hall, and they're forming watches at the gates."

"They've risen?" It was always harder to believe good news than bad.

"The Normans blinded one of the hostages but that only made the citizens angry. It was a cruel act."

"They would not give the King's body back for burial and that is a warrior's right." This foreign brutality was not his conception of war. It should be fought between equals and according to long established custom. The Welsh had been different but they were a hill folk with poor weapons.

"Shall I get your shield?" Edgar repeated.

Poor Alfhelm's wife had almost been shut out of the

city; Frain's mocking "Now the Godwin reign is over we may have peace," still echoed in his ears, yet at the final moment his countrymen had made the right choice. It was so surprising that the smith stood gaping at his own yard, wondering how it could have happened? Then he noticed Edgar fingering an almost useless knife. "They stole your sword and this is no moment to be weaponless," he put Ulgar's blade into the youth's hands, "use it well if you see a Norman climbing up the wall but I've told you its history, check it daily for rust."

The soil was so hard that Eldred was tempted to give up digging a hole in the garden bed. It might be a tradition handed down throughout generations that a man buried his silver in case of a siege but as he leaned on his spade for a moment's rest, it seemed a stupid precaution on this winter night. If Exeter were sacked what chance was there that any of them would survive? He would be killed on the walls, Goda would be carried away, Elfleda's possessions would be looted and if she were spared, the most she could expect was to tramp the roads until some farmer took her, out of charity, for a bondswoman. It was foolish to waste his strength on this present task when he was longing to return to his fireside and sleep. The day, just over, had seemed as long as a month. First he had stood for hours beside the Frisian, watching the fugitives from the neighboring villages drive their flocks inside the city; then there had been the terror of the attempted surrender of the town and the exultation afterwards when the people had risen and defied the Duke. Yet the fears of autumn were now facts. The enemy was barely half a mile away and he had watched the lanterns of the messengers catching the long legs and the pointed hoods of soldiers as they moved about their camp at dusk. It was not entirely a Norman army. The Duke had called out the English thanes who had submitted to his rule to save their lands. It must have been a hard decision for a man to make. He would have tried to reach whoever had raised the banner of resistance but a farmer thought naturally of his dependents and his cattle. Besides, and he remembered uneasily his own experiences on the border, it was difficult for any region to understand its neighbor. There was a gulf between Wessex with its woods and half wild shepherds and the richer, flatter meadows of his birthplace.

Eldred drove his spade deeper into the earth but light and sandy as it was, there had been some frost and he had to chip rather than dig. What had started this impulse to convert the wealth he possessed into silver during the previous summer? A vague idea of flight? No, as far as he could remember, this had not crossed his mind. Even now, the coins barely filled a small leather bag. He had had to buy meal, more than was customary because of the unsettled state of the land, there had been those gifts to the officials that Goda had wasted through her obstinacy, and the price of the iron that he needed for his work had increased. He discounted rumor when talking with his friends and yet some feeling of anxiety had driven him to make weapons instead of tools and convert his earnings into a form he could carry. He had expected an invasion, if it came, to be in May but outwardly, perhaps for Elfleda's sake, he had laughed at the idea although it had always lurked below the surface of his thoughts.

At last the hole was deep enough! He slipped the bag into an earthenware pot to keep the leather from spoiling and as he planted it (precisely like a bush) inside the hiding place another memory flashed across his head. How strange, how complicated the answers were, to the problems of a man's life. Where was Kynan? What had become of him? Ever since he had found Edgar starving among the trees, he kept thinking of the cave where he had waited so impatiently for the boy to wriggle back to him up the cliffs. Had Kynan inherited his father's headship and was he still living warily in his mountain village? The border had been quiet during the last few years, there were rumors that the offensive had passed to the Welsh. Still he might have been killed in some foray or have tumbled off a rock looking for a goat. "If I am spared," the smith began to shovel earth over the bowl with great strokes, "if I am spared, I am going back to Hereford." It was this that he wanted, this was the wish that had made him convert his earnings into easily carried coins, he longed to see the camps where he had once lived and smell the scent of cold bracken and twisted heather that was utterly different from the reeds and heavy grasses of the Exe. Something had always made him put off the journey or tried to prevent his even thinking of it; he had feared to leave Elfleda, duty had chained him to his forge, it had seemed a sin to spend his savings on so wild an expedition and yet a man had a right to take something for himself. He would fight now for the Godwins, without loyalty he could see no meaning in life, but if he lived through this siege, he stamped down the earth and scattered a few loose grains of soil over the top so that nobody would notice that the ground had been disturbed, yes, if he survived, he would buy a pony and ride northwest again, to see the mountains and look for Kynan, before he grew too old.

VI

It's mild, Master Frisian, for January."

"But damp." A sailor was more sensitive to the slightest shift of weather than a landsman and he could feel the threat of impending rain in the breeze.

"It will be difficult to keep the forge going next winter. They have cut the trees for five miles round." Eldred's preoccupation with timber for his work had become a legend in Exeter.

"Once they are defeated" (in his mind Thorkell was thinking *if*) "they ought to offer you two empty wagons free for a week after all the weapons you have mended, then you could go to the other side of Duryard for wood."

"Free! Can you see our Council with more than twenty farms ravaged and the parapets to repair, giving a citizen anything without payment? I sometimes feel they think I enjoy repairing axes."

"When you would rather be on the wall?" It was the fourth time since he had come on watch that Eldred had strolled down to stare over the battlements.

"Of course I would rather be on the wall. I was one of the Earl's housecarls."

He jerked his cloak round him with his left arm as if to prove that he could do everything but swing an axe. "They haven't troubled us much for the last three days. I believe they are getting tired."

"Maybe." The Duke was planning some trick, of that Thorkell was convinced, unless he were waiting for a fresh stock of arrows, but even with Eldred, it was wiser to keep his opinions to himself. Nobody was willing to listen to his advice, he was always "that foreigner," although he was one of the few men inside the city who had had experience of fighting overseas. He stared across the barren, trampled fields that led to the Norman camp. They were bare, with the curious faded green look that all grass had in winter, but the ground nearest the wall was covered with boulders that the citizens had flung against their assailants during the last attack. The invaders had carried away their dead but here and there, almost like bones, the stumps of burned out torches lay among the weeds.

It was so far away that they could only make out a blur of small figures wandering outside the mound of earth that the Normans had heaped up round their tents. "What are they doing there? They're too quiet," Thorkell regretted even so ordinary a comment as he made it but to his surprise, the smith nodded. "Yes, they're like the Welsh. As long as we could see them slipping from one bush to the other, we felt safe. It was when the land seemed empty that we looked to our weapons."

"What do you think is going to happen?"

"They're arguing. This is the first time that the Duke has met with a proper defense and he doesn't know whether to retire to Winchester or send for more men."

"They say there are English in his army."

"He called out those thanes who submitted to him and they had to bring their followers. I hope their lands are wasted as a punishment for their treachery."

Yet it was hard for a man who had only a small inheritance. He and his villagers would starve if they lost their land, their seed corn and their oxen. Nor was Thorkell convinced that the Normans despaired of their situation although there had been only a ritual throwing of stones against the walls and a few arrow shots recently; perhaps the Duke intended to starve them out? He looked across the plain at the great, imperial banner floating above the tents, it was the only spot of color in the winter landscape, and wondered how long their stocks of food would last? The townspeople had their stores but there were hundreds of fugitives in Exeter who had escaped with only what they could carry. "I shall be glad to come off watch, Eldred, and warm myself at the fire. The four hours this morning have seemed like a day."

"You haven't long to wait, I can hear the relief marching down the street. But you're right, I always hated the dawn watch when I was on the border, still you've got the day now before you're due on guard again. And I must get back to my forge."

———

This dust came from the stones they hurled. Most of the fighting was round the North Gate at the other end of the city but even so the shelf where Elfleda kept the drinking bowls was covered again with a gray, powdery layer although she had cleaned it once that morning. "What's the use?" Mildburh had said when she had run in as she always did to see that they had come safely through the night, "The town will be in ruins before the week's out." She was usually as gloomy in speech as she was cheerful in behavior.

It was habit, Elfleda supposed, pushing her cloth into a crack, although it was surely a wife's duty to keep the room in good order so that when a man came back from his turn of duty there was a familiar place where he could forget his anxieties and rest. Besides, it helped her to keep calm if she were busy; the mornings were easier to bear than the nights with the splintering sound of missiles hurtling against the parapets. Worst of all, how she dreaded it, was the hiss of an arrow as daylight came and wondering if it had found its mark in some poor wretch's body or if, as she prayed, had missed it? It was then she clutched the fleeces with both hands lest her shivering wake Eldred. Yet if she stopped to sort out her fears in her mind, it was less the present than the future that so terrified her. Whatever they said, it was possible for a night attack to succeed and she might wake to hear the Duke's men tramping down the streets, setting fire to the thatched roofs, slaying the old men and the un-armed serfs, and dragging Goda off with them in spite of anything she might do to save her daughter. She wondered if she had had some premonition of this as a child?

She had been so terrified when they told stories of sieges that she had clapped her hands to her ears and run away, even though they had laughed at her. Now she, Goda, Mildburh, all the women inside Exeter had to endure, nobody knew for how long, and to add to her anxiety Eldred was always finding some excuse to slip away to the battlements. One day he would go there once too often and the townsmen would bring him back to her door with his head crushed in by a boulder.

It was time to start cooking their meal but where had her daughter disappeared? The serving woman had gone on an errand and somebody must fetch the water that they were allowed to draw, morning and evening. "Goda!" Where could the child be hiding? There was no washing now to hang up in the orchard and she had forbidden the girl to leave the house. "Goda!" She felt her voice turn into a shriek. "But I'm here, Mother," came a cross answer from behind her, "shaking out the dusters in the courtyard as you ordered."

"Take the pail, will you, and get our water. I dare not leave the fire. You know what your stepfather is like, he counts every twig he gives us."

"We have less wood than any of our neighbors and he has two enormous piles for his forge."

"Don't chatter at the well. I need the water at once." It was an exaggeration, she had enough to cook their broth, but she would never have sent her daughter to such a spot alone if it had not been for the siege. It was unsuitable for a young girl to linger there, listening to gossips who had nothing better to do than to exchange rumors, all equally untrue, with any stranger or silly serving maid who would listen to them.

"I won't be long." Goda took the pail from its hook and started briskly up the road. As long as the bucket was empty, the walk was a pleasant change, besides it showed that her elders realized that she was now grown up. Her mother could say what she pleased, the siege was not as bad as those four dreadful months that she had spent in attendance upon the old Queen. Then every day had been an exercise in misery, a trap closing down that had shut her off from her friends and the cheerful, busy life of her own neighborhood into a gray, hardly believable existence governed by continual prayers and her step-father's harsh command, "You will stay for at least a year." She had tried to remember the warm kitchen of her home when kneeling behind the Queen's ladies in a dark church, her hands tingling with chilblains and her ears numb with cold. Everything she had said or done had been a sin for which they had scolded her. It was better to be shut up inside Exeter because although it might be alarming when the yells began at night, at least she was with friends, with her mother who fetched an extra cloak to throw about her shoulders when the fire died almost out and joked with them all because there was only half a portion of porridge. Besides, her step-father said that they were safe from the Normans and he had been a soldier and should know. She was free, this was the first time that she had been sent alone to the well and she could not honestly say that she was either fright-ened or unhappy.

The sun was out and there was hardly any wind. Her thoughts jumped to spring, would the Duke's men leave before it was time to scatter through the meadows and collect the cowslip roots that her mother dried and boiled in milk to cure the winter coughs? Actually she preferred the draught that Cousin Mildburh made. She steeped hers in ale and heated it until it almost burned the chest as it was swallowed.

There were several women already at the well, some had filled their buckets but it was an opportunity to chatter and they were in no hurry to go back to their kitchens, "What difference does it make who is our master?" The thin sullen looking woman next in line rested her pail on the stone rim of the fountain. "Life will go on the same for us whoever it is now. King Harold is dead and Wessex lost."

"And our fields are ravaged, where will the bread come from next summer?"

"We ought to yield and beg for mercy before those fugitives eat up our stores."

"Why should we surrender when we've beaten back every attack?" Goda was too quick tempered to conceal her feelings and she recognized the last speaker. The woman came from a house in the next street that belonged to one of the thanes who had negotiated with the Duke.

"Ah! Her mother has sent her lamb to fetch the water instead of keeping her by her side." An older woman in a greasy apron stared insolently at the girl. "Dame Elfleda," she made the name sound like an insult, "knows you are going to be some archer's prize so it doesn't matter now if you hear a truth or two from us."

"No Norman will set foot inside Exeter."

"It's easy to boast when your father is never on the walls."

"He's a smith!" It was particularly unjust to repeat lies about her stepfather. Everybody knew that it was impossible to keep him away from the North Gate.

"Oh, don't provoke the child!" The thin woman, having filled her pail, stepped between them. "She's a poor little Godwin serving maid—or was. The Queen dismissed you, didn't she?" She lifted her hand as if to push Goda away and the girl slapped her.

"Take that!" An onlooker flung a pot of water in Goda's face, "It will calm you down."

"Aren't you ashamed! Why are you standing here when the men are coming back for their meal?" Edgar came up unexpectedly, swinging his leather headpiece by its strap, he was just off watch.

"They want to give in, they want to give in, they are traitors, all of them," Goda sobbed, trying to wipe the water from her cheeks. At least it was clean, it could have been slops. "They said my father was afraid to fight." She noticed she had said father instead of stepfather but did not correct herself.

"Then I'm glad you hit one." Edgar looked round but the women were already in flight, one, her skirts flying, was halfway up the road, the others were disappearing into a garden. He took Goda's pail, filled it for her although this was a woman's job, and beckoned her to follow him. "Never mind what they say," he muttered gruffly, "there are always cowards in every town."

"What's the news?" It was all she could think of to say, her dress was soaked and the cold air was driving through it onto her skin as if it were a prickly bramble but she wasn't going to let Edgar or anyone else think that she cared.

"It's quiet. We suspect they're preparing to leave."

"Then should we be able to go outside again?" She was still wondering about the cowslip roots.

"I think the gates would be shut for a while. We should harry the army on their retreat."

"Why?" To Goda, once the army was a day's march away, it meant that Exeter was safe.

"Any live Norman is a danger to us. We shall hunt them like rats till Wessex is ours again." Even if he could never hear the familiar shout of "Edgar" and his father's footsteps crossing the yard he would have avenged him; the silver drops would still glisten along the trees beside the river, and there were things that even the invaders could not change.

"I supposed once they were driven away we should have peace." The woods round Exeter had been Goda's boundaries as long as she could remember and Winchester or Edgar's home were the shadows of a story told round a flickering fire.

"It would only be a beginning." As far as Duke William was concerned, Edgar knew, there could never be an ending to his hatred. Yet it was natural for a girl as young as Goda to be anxious, she was still so near childhood that it was easy to talk to her. "There would be plenty of citizens left in Exeter," he wanted to reassure her, "and your stepfather would not leave his forge."

"And you would go with them?" For no special reason a memory flashed through her head of a falconer's boy in a tawny red jerkin much too short for him but with a speckled feather in his cap that he must have picked up in some wood, who had brought a message to the Queen's household. While he was waiting for an answer, turning an old leather hawking glove over and over in his hands, he had looked up suddenly and smiled at her. It had brought the happy, outside world from which she had been banished directly into the drafty passage where they stood and she had thought about him all day. Now, as she watched Edgar, carrying what she could hardly lift as easily as if it were an empty basket, he reminded her of the youth, although it was the first time that she had put the two impressions together.

"I have my father to avenge." Goda would have liked to tell him how sorry she was but the right words would not come. They passed the apple trees in Cousin Mildburh's garden, they were at the wattle fence that surrounded the forge, if only she could say something to soften her mother's sharpness, it was strange that she hated Edgar so much, but almost as if they had run there, they were at her own door without her even thanking him. "I will take the bucket now," she put out her hand but it was too late, her mother had seen them. "What is this, Goda, it was you I sent to the well," then she saw her daughter's dripping dress, "what has happened?"

"It was those idle women from thane Eadnoth's house. Like their master, they want to surrender Exeter." A little water splashed over Edgar's dusty shoes as he set the bucket down inside the kitchen.

"They threw a pail of water over me."

"You must have provoked them, Goda, and I thought I could trust you." She had been so careful and now the neighbors would nudge one another and whisper, "Did you see the girl? She was walking back from the fountain with that Sussex runaway." Elfleda looked up the street and sure enough, the head of a serving woman ducked behind Mildburh's hedge. "You should have come straight home and I would have gone back with you myself."

An icy trickle was creeping down Goda's back and the fire was too small for her to dry herself properly. "But how could I be silent when they said such dreadful things about us?" Her mother turned coldly away and Goda burst out crying again, "But they started first, I was waiting in line and I didn't do anything wrong. Why must you always scold me?"

It was wise to spend a few hours comfortably in front of a fire. True, there was the smoke but to be really warm for part of the day was a bulwark to endurance. Many people had only a few sticks left to heat their bowls of meal and went back to the ramparts still shivering from their last guard. "Always keep a little more, Thorkell, than you think you will need." It had been his uncle's first lesson and a good one. He had bought a load of logs the previous autumn and still had enough to heat the room and have his men cooked hot meals for another couple of months. Yet tonight he felt uneasy. He could have given Eldred no particular reason if the smith had been sitting opposite on the other stool. The walls were solid and as long as they did not let themselves be tempted into the fields where the archers would pick them off like a flock of little birds, Exeter could hold out for weeks. There was even enough food if it could be shared out properly. The citizens had their stocks but the wretched villagers who had fled before the Duke had had only what they could carry. The city doled them out a little bread but it was not enough to make soldiers of them. It was foolish to be so anxious, he had been in too many battles to tremble like a boy. All the same, as he might have said aboard the *Seabird*, "It may be a blue sky now but it will be blowing a nor'easter before sundown."

The warmth made him drowsy and he drifted first into a half conscious sleep and then into that recurrent nightmare from his second voyage that returned at times to haunt him. Just as now, at the changing of the watch, a raider had slipped out of the mist and glided towards them. "Looking for slaves," his uncle had said bitterly, stamping the deck in anger. They had put on sail but the vessel had drawn nearer and nearer. He had felt for his knife but a sailor had sworn at him, "Don't throw it away. They are more likely to cut our throats if we have nothing to give them." Then he had stared into the trough of the waves and wondered if he should jump? They had watched the ship gaining on them for nearly an hour and then, the crew had sworn it was a miracle, the fog had thickened suddenly and under its cover, minding neither currents nor unknown rocks, they had slid away. The fright had marked him and well, it was no use laughing at a sailor's beliefs, the memory had recurred whenever a change was likely in his affairs. It had come before his uncle's death, it had floated into his head before the great storm when the *Seabird* had lost her mast. He shivered as he woke, and he threw another log onto the fire, wastefully because in a few moments the bell would ring to summon them back on watch.

Why were the Normans so quiet? He did not believe they would retreat, not with the bribe of the rich pastures and orchards surrounding the city. Perhaps they were waiting for some change inside Exeter? The faction for surrender was growing as supplies grew less and casualties more numerous. A split among the citizens of a beleaguered town was far more dangerous than the arrival of a few reinforcements.

"It's time," Osmund tapped on the door, came abruptly into the room and walked over to the hearth to warm his hands. His head in its tightly fitting leather cap, half in shadow and half lit by the flames, really looked like a seal's muzzle, bobbing between two waves.

"It's harder to turn out ashore than aboard ship."

"One's as bad as the other."

Thorkell yawned. He ought to get up but his mind seemed to have lost its power to influence his limbs and he lingered drowsily, still under the spell of his dream. He looked from corner to corner of the room, it was the charter of his life. The Frisian cloak that a cousin had given him was hanging from its peg, the two Irish glasses were safely on their high shelf (he had bartered a roll of cloth for them and a hard bargain it had been!), if he stretched his hand out he could touch the chest where his uncle's bone-scratched charts, as valuable to a merchant as his ship, were safely covered by the blue, embroidered jerkin that he wore only if summoned before the Council or at the Christmas feast.

"It's time," Osmund repeated uneasily, stamping the fresh log out with his heavy boot. It had not had time to catch properly alight. He stared at Thorkell as if he feared that his master was sick.

A moment more . . . a moment more . . . peace would vanish when he moved but pride drove the merchant finally to his feet. He grabbed an old sea cape that was stiff with salt and joined the men waiting impatiently for him in the courtyard.

It was a cold, quiet night with nothing to do but to trudge up and down and by the time that Eldred reached the battlements for a final inspection before going back to his house, most of the watch had assembled round a brazier skillfully hidden behind an angle of the wall so that its glow would not draw an arrow into their midst, although it was unlikely that an archer would risk a shaft in such darkness. There was little talk, the men longed for sleep and it was the moment when, as the smith knew, the surrender party gained fresh adherents. The fools! They had only to hold out for another couple of weeks and their assailants would be obliged to retreat for lack of food. It was known that the Duke had lost a lot of his horsemen and supplies in the neighborhood of the camp must be exhausted. The tracks in winter were no place for any wagon. It amused Eldred to think how many must be stranded up to their axles in mud. Bread could be reaching the army only on the backs of men or, to a small extent, on ponies. Yes, Exeter held the fortunes of the West in its grasp and one day, not so far off, they would wake to see the smoke rising from the ruins of the Norman camp and the Duke himself in full retreat towards Winchester.

"Still awake, Master Frisian?" His friend was staring so intently over the parapet that for a moment Eldred wondered if he were sleeping on his feet.

"They are so quiet, it makes me uneasy."

"If they were planning a night attack, we should hear them bringing up the ladders."

"Perhaps," Thorkell drew his fingers along the stone slab in front of him as if testing its strength, "but I can't help thinking about a story I heard on my last voyage to Flanders."

"Tell me about it, it may keep me awake." Eldred was not part of the watch, being a smith and having other duties, but he was ashamed to go back to his warm kitchen, while his friends were on guard.

Thorkell hesitated. He had learned as a boy to keep the details of his journeys to himself or people called him a liar, not realizing that a man who faced more rocks, sandbanks and currents than he could ever learn, had to stick to facts. Still, Eldred had fought for three years on the border and had a wider view than his fellow citizens, many of whom had never been twenty miles from their homes. "If Normandy had not been ravaged during his childhood, the Duke would never have invaded us. His vassals drew so little from their lands they were becoming restless."

" 'Little seeds, great harvests,' as the country people say, but go on with your story."

"They were besieging a castle, I can't remember if it was in Normandy or France, anyhow the place held out for days. Then they drove a mine under one of the walls and took it easily."

"A mine?" Eldred had heard the word but it had no clear meaning for him, it was like a phrase, every harper had a dozen of them, linking up the edges of a story.

"They dug a passage underground until they were close to the battlements. Then they stuffed brushwood and timber into the hole and set it alight. The stones cracked, the wall collapsed and they dashed through the breach."

"But the defenders must have heard them!"

"Apparently it was a complete surprise."

"It could happen to a small castle with a few soldiers. But here," Eldred swung his arm round in a circle to indicate the towers, the churches and the parapets that would be visible in daylight, "all the citizens would be waiting for them."

"I heard the tale as well from one of the attackers," Osmund had come over to join them, his cloak drawn round him so tightly that it looked like a rolled sail, "but the earth has to be light. If it's heavy, with pebbles in it, you hear the spades."

"Don't frighten us," Thorkell tried to make a joke of it, "our soil is little better than sand."

Eldred nodded, strange things, he knew, happened on the other side of the Channel but of course it had been fatigue. They had kept no proper watch. Godric had once trapped some Welsh inside a cave and smoked them out but such incidents conflicted with his ideas of war. A battle was the shield wall, the swinging axes, eventually swords. It was not archers hidden behind hummocks and shooting at a man's undefended head nor diggers burrowing underneath the grass. Exeter was full of men, it was only a question of endurance, of never letting the will to resist slacken for a moment. "I hope this is not going to delay your summer expedition?" He did not want to hurt his friend's feelings by seeming to doubt his tale.

"We made as many preparations as we could before the *Seabird* was laid up for the winter."

"Otherwise this will be your third voyage?"

"As captain, yes, my fifth if I count the twice I was out with my uncle."

"So they will give you a thane's rank on your return."

"I shall be a citizen of Exeter." It did not matter that his uncle had brought him here when he was two and that he had grown up among the boats along the Exe; until he had made three voyages as owner of his ship, he was tolerated as a foreign merchant but not accepted as a native. Citizen of Exeter. He rolled the words round on his tongue without actually repeating them. "It's a temptation, Eldred, if we chase the Duke as far as Winchester, I may have to fret through another winter before we can sail."

So much could happen, a stray arrow, a storm, some sandbank that had shifted since they had last turned south, it was better not to dream about a wish till some of the perils were over. "It's eighteen days," he said with a yawn, "I must cut a further notch on my tally stick in the morning."

"Another hour . . ." either they were growing accustomed to the darkness or it had become a little lighter. Nothing had happened, nothing would happen but the two facts: the Normans were outside in their camp, they were shivering inside on their walls. Reality became the bitter midnight cold that made a leather coat feel like a spider's web. Eldred walked up and down, twenty paces forward, twenty paces back. One of the men beside the brazier smiled at him as he passed, as if asking for reassurance or help. The Frisian continued to stare towards the fields, Osmund gently stamped his feet. It was so peaceful that Eldred wondered if it were really wise to keep so many on guard? They would fight better after a sound sleep. He wished he had come for the morning watch, his city was so beautiful in the daylight when the light crept up the spires as if they were trees, bare of leaf in January but dappled with silver. How quiet it was, this was the night silence that he had known in Wales but that many people had never experienced in their lives because when the curfew sounded, they hurried to their own hearths. How still . . . how silent . . . a pause when even the earth held its breath.

A roar rose into the sky as if it would tear the heaven itself into bits. Something cracked, a giant from an elder age was smiting the ground with a hammer, stones smashed, there were yells from outside the ditch, dust filled their noses and eyes, one crash succeeded the other. "The wall," Osmund yelled, "they've mined the wall, it's our own soil that has betrayed us."

VII

Dawn had come. Eldred had let the fire go out, it was useless to sharpen weapons any longer, the Council had ordered the watch to their homes and had sent their heralds to beg for peace. He sat in front of his forge, exhausted but unable to sleep, with his hood pulled forward over his ears. This would be the spot he would remember when the Normans dragged him away, not the scarlet of Godric's pennant nor the gold October of the Welsh hills, but the gray, dismal mornings (not unlike the day that was beginning now) when his father had sent him out to add a stick or rake out a log that was burning too fiercely while his blood was calling him out to the wild moors. *"The exact heat."* How he still rebelled at the words! He ground his foot in a useless gesture against a pan of cold ashes that stood near his stool and yet knew that this moment, this dreadful moment when the Duke's men might storm across the threshold to stab him, plunder his house and turn his family out to beg, was not as terrifying as the hours that he had waited here, at just this same turning of the light, to come to a youth's strength so that he could slip away to the border. For he had been happy once he had reached Godric, the years with the housecarls had fulfilled all he had asked of life. Then, as he caught sight of the yard that his wife had seen was regularly swept, he felt guilty at having forgotten about her. Poor Elfleda! She was waiting in the kitchen, fearing more for her daughter than for the possessions that she had guarded for him so carefully, anxious perhaps, lest his own arrogance ruin them directly he saw a Norman. She was afraid, he thought grimly, of corpses. And still it need not have happened. The cowards! He longed to fling a lighted torch against the Council Hall roof, to watch it burn with all the grasping thanes inside it who were submitting the West to foreign rule merely to save a portion of their lands when if he had had his way, they would have fought on, shoulder to shoulder, shield touching shield, inside the breach.

"Eldred!" The voice was familiar enough but he was too exhausted and angry to reassure even a neighbor. Sack or submission, the known followers of the Godwins would be handed over immediately to the Duke's vengeance.

"Eldred!"

"How can I help you, Thorkell, we must wait for what has to happen. There is nothing else we can do."

"Oh, but there is." The smith could not know that the happiness that flashed across the Frisian's face was because Eldred had called him by his own name for almost the first time. "I waited outside the Council Hall for Frain to leave. The Duke has proposed terms for sparing the city and there will be no fighting while a deputation goes to his camp but it is only a matter of hours. The Queen and the Godwins are hurrying to the river and the foreign merchants will leave with them so I have come to offer you and your household a place on my ship."

"You are putting to sea? In winter?"

"It will make a January tale for our descendants. The wind is in the right direction and there are several ports further along the coast. You can decide later on whether you want to remain in Cornwall or come on with me to Milford."

"Thorkell!" He could not say more but shook the merchant violently by the hand.

"Go first and speak to Frain. He is your neighbor and he may be able to look after your house. Bring your tools, as much food as you can carry and tell your wife to take plenty of fleeces, it is going to be cold. But you must be at the *Seabird* within an hour. My men are busy getting her ready for sea and once the Queen has sailed, we dare not wait."

"It's life . . ." Eldred stammered, fate was sweeping him away from the forge a second time and he looked round the yard without sorrow.

"It's exile and it's hardship but it's freedom." Thorkell glanced up at the house where he had spent so many winter hours, talking about his voyages, making plans for next spring. "Who knows? Perhaps all of us will come back here one day," yet as he said this he knew it was a lie.

It was some moments after Thorkell closed the gate behind him before the smith moved. He looked round the yard, at the metal fragments that the forge boy had swept up and put into an old basket in front of the wall and at the bare branches of the apple trees in the adjoining garden. To leave, never to see his home again, meant little to him if he weighed it against loyalty. "In an hour." There was Frain to see, the silver to dig up again from its hiding place, a choice to make among his stock of tools. Luckily he had sold most of his store of weapons at the beginning of the siege. "Elfleda!" He hurried towards the kitchen. "Elfleda!" She came running to meet him, astonished at the cheerfulness in his voice. Had they arranged a truce? Would life go on as before except that they would be poorer after the fines and tribute had been paid?

"They are surrendering the city but Thorkell has offered us a passage on the *Seabird*. The Queen and the Godwins are leaving by ship."

There was a stone loose in the wall that now would never be replaced and what was the use of the coverlet that she had spent a year embroidering for Eldred if they had no bed? She looked back at the garden that had been her pride and for the first time since the fighting had begun, tears came into her eyes.

"Elfleda," it was harder for a woman to leave her home than a man, "they say the Duke had promised that no women or children shall be harmed. Stay here, Frain is your kinsman and he will see that neither Goda nor yourself come to any hurt."

It was a temptation for a moment. There had been months when she had struggled against her father's decision to marry her to Eldred. He had seen the outward, material possessions of the smith but not into his daughter's heart. Yet though she resented her husband's fanatical devotion to the Godwins, "One of their falcons means more to him than I do," they had come nearer to each other during the siege. He had been patient, protective of them all and full of a gaiety that she had never known in him before as if some inner anxiety had been lifted. Besides, it was a wife's duty to follow her husband and she had always clung to the principles that she had learned from her own mother. "I suppose it will be better to be drowned at sea than murdered here," she saw her words surprised Eldred, "besides, what made you think that I would leave you?"

"I do not know." This was a fact, perhaps because he was aloof himself, he had never tried to break down a certain remoteness in his wife. Besides, he was uncertain how far Elfleda, with her profound love for her native city, could face the uneasy, tormented existence of an exile. "It will be hard, harder for you than for me. Think well before you decide."

"The Duke's men know nothing of our language and our customs. How long will it be before everything we value is destroyed?"

"Food and fleeces then, they matter most, and now I must speak to the household." He saw only the practical details while she longed for a word, some special gesture of sympathy, before she closed the gate on her home. "Eldred!" She could not even take his arm because he was striding, several steps ahead of her, into the kitchen.

All the household was asleep except Goda; she had taken refuge in her mother's room. They woke up sleepily, tired by the siege to a point where they could hardly respond, perhaps barely understand, what Eldred was saying to them. His voice was sharp, as Godric's might have been, he knew that he was looking at them as a unity for the last time, the red cheeked oval of the forge boy's face reminded him of the messengers who had brought news into the camp to warn them of a minor raid. "The Duke offers his peace to all who will swear him loyalty but I am leaving with the Godwins by sea. You are free to stay here and join another master or come with me as you wish."

"I will serve you faithfully, wages or no wages," as he had anticipated Edgar stepped forward almost before he had finished speaking, "what have I to expect from the Normans but hunger?"

"Then help my wife, she is packing up the food. And you?" The three others seemed stunned by the news.

"I would go," the forge boy was the next to answer, "but my mother is old and I cannot leave her." It was the right decision and Eldred smiled at him.

"Oh, my mistress!" The serving woman burst into a loud wail. "I shall never find so good a lady again but those waves, those terrible waves . . ." She flung her apron over her head as if to blot out all thought of them.

"And what will you do, Merewin?" The man was staring at the bundle of rushes from which he had just scrambled up as if he had not heard the smith's words. Surely his face had not been so wrinkled nor his hair so gray before the siege? "I do not want to be a burden to you," it seemed an effort for him to speak, "but I think I can hammer out a metal ring for another few years. Besides, I was born on one of Queen Gytha's farms."

"Come then and welcome. Take the boy and get our tools together but leave everything broken here."

There was a pause. It was as if they were bracing themselves to face a gale that would meet them on the other side of some hill. Then there was a wail outside, the noise of some messenger running by, a rumble as if stones had fallen again and finally an ominous silence. "Hurry," he clapped Merewin on the shoulder, "pack what you can and follow me to the river. You must all help me to get the bales to the *Seabird*, Master Thorkell expects to sail in an hour."

"I must see Frain, I must see Frain," the words ran through the smith's mind as he strapped on his sword and slung the bag of silver that he had just dug up over his shoulder. There was so much to do, there was so little time, the moments that had been as sluggish as a frozen pond on the night watch, were galloping away as fast as an Earl's horse. "Take what you have prepared and start," he strode through the kitchen where knives, hammers, coats and sacks of meal were piled in confusion around the door, "wait for me beside Master Thorkell's men, I will join you shortly at the ship."

There was no need to go as far as his neighbor's house. Frain pushed open the gate and came towards him as if the Normans were already on his heels. "Eldred! Eldred! Whatever are you doing? Go yourself if you must but leave Elfleda here."

"She has chosen to come with me."

"How can you take a woman on a winter voyage and into some lawless camp for the sake of a leader you saw once and then only from a distance?"

Yet it was not merely the Godwins, although now if ever they needed his loyalty, it was England. Had his fellow citizens lost all memory? What of the fighting in the North? It was the losses at Stamford that had turned the battle by Hastings into a defeat. Why were those facts, so clear to him, banished as utterly as a common outlaw from the minds of Exeter's citizens?

"I told Elfleda she was free to stay. I will not swear obedience to a foreigner and you know this, Frain, but my wife is your cousin and if she wishes, I will leave her with her kinsfolk."

"There is no shaking your obstinacy," Frain stared across the yard towards the burned out fire of the forge. How could a man leave his livelihood and his possessions, couldn't he see that nothing, nothing, nothing, could bring the Godwins to power again? "But why do you speak as if we have been beaten here? We shall have to pay tribute, yes, but we paid it to King Edward while he was alive. Once we open our gates, there is to be no looting and no reprisals."

"Wait a year and see what the Duke does then."

"Go yourself if you must but leave your wife. I will treat her as part of my family."

"I know you would, Frain," they had not heard Elfleda's approaching steps, "but I prefer to follow my husband. I must say goodbye to Mildburh"; for once, but she did not notice this, she was giving them orders, "but start the others towards the ship, it is getting late. And now, come with me, cousin. I must talk to you about the house."

There was so many directions to give as they hurried up the road that she barely noticed Frain's angry words about stupidity and recklessness. She now saw as clearly as Eldred, if from another angle, that flight was the only path open to them. The first time that a Norman jeered at her husband, he would take him by the throat and then they would all be lost. Even if it were only herself, she had no wish to see the army that had mangled her countryside and killed her friends, take possession of the city. She was so sure that she had made the right decision that as Mildburh came to meet her, she noticed that her friend had put on her brown and yellow striped dress back to front in her haste. It made her look much broader than she actually was.

"Elfleda! You cannot go. You know you are welcome here although I see no reason why you cannot stay on in your own house, but you will die, I know you will, if you join that ship."

"I am leaving with Eldred."

"But your duty is over if he leaves his birthplace! Besides you never loved him."

"Perhaps not at first but I do now. He needs me."

"And Goda?"

"Goda! I shall never understand the child. Sometimes I think she spends her time thinking of how she can annoy me. I gave her the choice because I knew you would have taken her into your household but she cried and insists on coming with us."

They were a long way from the actual breach but Mildburh had screamed in terror when they had heard the noise of the cracking walls. She would never forget the hours that she waited beside a handful of fire, trying not to cry in front of her maidservants but wondering if she would wander begging through the countryside before the week was over? Then Frain had come back saying that there was to be peace, she had been so happy, she had planned to rush over and tell her friend the news and yet now, looking up, she saw, not her childhood companion, but a stranger. They had picked their berries together every autumn, they had exchanged thoughts that they had hidden even from themselves while hanging their linen up to dry, and now it was to end in mystery. She might never hear if the *Seabird* had reached another port. "Oh, Fleda, surely I'm worth as much as that half crippled man who shouts at you when you have done more for him than a mother? Don't let him take you away from me."

"He said I should choose. I go of my own free will."

"You can't, Fleda, you can't. Don't you remember sitting on a bank and telling me that your father wanted you to remarry so that there was a husband to look after your property when he died? It was the house that he was thinking of, not Eldred."

"Yes, it will be six years next April." She remembered the meadow. The Normans had camped upon that particular spot and rooted the flowers out with their nailed shoes. She would not want to see the place again now that they had defiled it. "I brought this for you although it isn't finished," she pushed a heavy bundle into Mildburh's hands, "I was embroidering it for you for Easter and there's a dress of mine as well. It's old but may be useful for the garden. But do one favor for me. Send your serving woman over to fetch my spinning wheel when I have left. I've used it so long I should like to think it was here and not being kicked about by strangers."

"Oh, Fleda!" Mildburh could not help looking greedily at a projecting edge of the cloth and, of course, if Eldred persisted in this madness, there was that bulge at the bottom of the fence that really belonged to their own orchard, but she must not have such thoughts when her friend was going towards a probable death. "You must stay here. Your father would have ordered you not to leave."

"Frain is my kinsman. Tell him to sell the house if he can. Some Norman will be your neighbor if it stands there empty."

"Men are crazy . . . crazy . . ."

"No, it is the Duke who is to blame. He has harried the country so as to give the lands of the English he has slain to his own mercenaries."

"Don't go, don't go."

"I must, Mildburh. Think of me when you go out to the moors in the spring. And who knows, one day, when the city is settled again, perhaps I can come back, if only for a visit." A bell rang somewhere, was that a signal to the ships, she kissed her friend hurriedly and ran up the street, it was still some distance to the river.

Eldred, as he sat on a ledge at the end of the road, wondered if his wife really intended to join him? She had said she would come, he had been astonished at her choice yet perhaps their quarrel over Goda had resolved something, a woman always wanted her way, but the girl was now less quarrelsome and he still felt that although she had only been for a few months with the Queen, the experience had tamed her. Tamed? The word reminded him of the falcons that meant so much to Harold's sons. If only they had thought a little less of hawking and more about driving the Duke out of the West!

Where was Elfleda? It was almost full daylight. He looked down the street but it was empty and Thorkell had warned him that he could not wait. How still it was after the tumult of the last few days. The thatched roof on his right was gray with dust, an ivy leaf had forced itself through the bright green moss on a broken stone. He would not have noticed it if he had been hurrying along upon some errand. Was his wife coming or not? Surely she would not let him wait like this if she had changed her mind? He was about to walk back to see what had happened when he saw her coming towards him, a bundle tucked against her side and a heavy basket grasped in her left hand.

"I would not let the others come with me. Frain was angry and Mildburh did nothing but cry."

"But the basket's too heavy for you," he recognized it as the one he had bought from Alfhelm, "your kinsman could have carried it as far as the ship. But give it to me, I will take it."

"You can't, your hands are full," she laughed as if they were merely strolling off to market together, "what a bundle you've made. How do you expect to get that through the crowd?"

He had determined to show them that he could carry things even if he had a crippled elbow, besides everything that they could save would double in value by the time they reached some distant port. So he had slung a bag of meal across his shoulder, the heavy silver was strapped to his belt and his extra garments and a couple of knives that he had not sold were rolled up inside a fleece. "This is the best way," he turned down a winding alley, "it's narrow and a little longer but we shall avoid the throngs."

There were few visible indications of the siege in this quarter of the city. The Exe had protected it and only the shut doors and the absence of women sweeping their yards marked any change from an ordinary day. It would have been different if the smith had returned to the part of the wall where he had spent the previous night and looked from it at a countryside that he was probably leaving for ever. There he would have seen burned roofs with, underneath, the litter of battle: an arrow head buried in a wattle fence, the half of a broken weapon, stone chips and rings from a coat of mail, scattered together over the frozen earth. There were still men on guard when they came to the West Gate, tired (who wasn't tired in Exeter that morning?), wrapped in cloaks and leaning on their axes.

"Master Eldred!" One of the Frisian's sailors stepped forward and took Elfleda's basket. "I was beginning to be afraid I had missed you. Your household has reached the *Seabird* safely but I was sent to bring you across the marshes. We shall never reach the boat if we keep to the road."

"Hurry, if you are bound for the ships. No one is to pass once the Godwin party is here."

Hurry! It was what everyone was trying to do but the area between the city and the river was full of people trying to escape by sea. Men jostled each other on the narrow paths, glancing behind them and then yelling at friends as abusively as if they were Normans, cursing as a fleece slipped from between their frozen fingers and somebody's possessions were scattered over the frozen track so that cups, jerkins and loaves of bread had to be scooped up and knotted into a pack again or stumbling and banging into each other in the slime until the shouting, angry mob came to a standstill.

It was not far to the ships but at first they were caught inside a row of people and Elfleda wondered if she had stayed too long with Mildburh and her kinsman? She could feel Eldred's anxiety as he walked beside her. Yet how could she rush out of her house without saying a word to Frain about its future or bidding goodbye to her friend? A wind was lifting her hood that she had not had time to fasten properly, the pack on the man's shoulders in front of her bobbed up and down in front of her eyes. Otherwise she would have felt that she was living through a nightmare from which she would wake gratefully, it seemed impossible that twelve hours ago she had been cooking their supper and measuring the meal left in the jar and that today she was hurrying towards a foreign land. "Now!" The sailor, pushing and dodging, managed to lead them out of the crowd and along a damp meadow where it was possible to move. "It's wet but we shall get to a track again over there, it's not much further than the road."

"Coming with us, mother?" The smith joked as an angry and flustered old woman came to the door of a little hut and stared at them.

"Coming? Why? The fighting has stopped and that is all that matters. It's the same to me whether a Duke or an Earl rules Exeter. Men want eggs and I know how to hide them till they pay me. They burned down Osgeat's dwelling," she glanced round savagely at the city, "they said it might shelter the archers. But the Normans never came this way and now who will build it up again? Osgeat is a good man, you cannot say it is a judgment on him."

"The Queen would have helped him. It was the Council that surrendered."

"Maybe, maybe," Eldred could see that she did not believe him and he was uncertain himself if the man would have had any compensation for his loss, "but the noise and the cold have killed many of my hens and since I could not go to the wood to collect my winter sticks, I have nothing for a fire. The Queen gave many alms and may God's blessing go with her but what do I care about the others? What changes can the Duke bring into my life? I am too poor."

Eldred thrust a small coin into her hand before he hurried after the others. They were now within sight of the *Seabird*, its crew were still carrying bales aboard but as they came nearer, stepping carefully across the swampy ground, they could see the rest of the household waiting for them on the path that ran along the top of the river bank.

The handle of a basket had marked her wrist and as she rubbed it Goda wondered why her mother was so late. Could she have decided to stay with their kinsfolk after all? For herself, the thought of change excited her, she wanted to go to places she had never seen and make new friends. It would be dreadful to slink back into Exeter, the city under a lot of Norman soldiers would never be the same, besides, she knew what would happen, her mother would never let her leave the house alone. How strange life was! She had still been asleep when Master Thorkell had come, they had shaken her awake saying, "Quick, dress, pack what you most need, we are leaving on the *Seabird* in an hour." Oh, what a confusion it had been! She had put on her warmest clothes and stuffed all she could into a basket but then they had given her the butter to carry, the jar must have been full, it was as heavy as a log, and at the last moment yelled at her not to forget her fleece. She had abandoned so many things and now, as the wind freshened, and she pulled her cloak more tightly round her, she noticed a gap at her throat. "My brooch, oh, my brooch! It's the one the Queen gave me when I left her service. It must still be at our house."

"Where?" Edgar was standing between her and the serving woman, a little in advance of Merewin and the boy.

"On the ledge in my room. I remember now, a skirt

was flopping out of my bundle and I pinned it together with the clasp I use every day. Then my belt wasn't big enough to go round the whole pack and while I was looking for a bit of rope, my stepfather called us." Now they would scold her for losing her most valuable possession but why had they hurried off so rapidly only to wait here for nearly an hour? If her mother had not dashed off to her kinsfolk, she would have gone through the rooms in an orderly fashion to see that nothing important had been forgotten. "Don't fret!" She turned round to see the serving woman looking at her mockingly, "He's gone back to fetch it." "Who?" She was puzzled for a moment, then she saw Edgar racing back towards Exeter and the woman laughed. Oh, how she longed to slap her face. Was she suggesting that the brooch had been left behind so that Edgar could do her a service or had the maid hoped to collect the pin for herself?

"Here we are," the smith's voice startled Goda because she had been trying to trace Edgar's running figure among the crowds in the field and had not expected her family to cross what seemed to her a dangerous swamp, "ready to go on board."

"Master Thorkell asks us to wait until he sends for us," Merewin stepped forward, proud to be the message bearer, "the *Seabird* is the last in line and can only sail when the Godwins have left."

Eldred glanced round the group, the two women were sitting on a large bundle, the forge boy was tying up a basket and Merewin was beside him, "Where is Edgar?" he asked.

Nobody replied. He looked along the row, counting

them again and then the serving woman answered with a laugh, "Oh, my young mistress left her brooch behind and he went back for it."

"He went back! Goda, is this true?" The girl ought to have stayed behind with her mother's kinsfolk, she was always a nuisance.

"I said, anybody could have heard me, I must have forgotten my brooch in my room but I never asked him, or anybody else, to fetch it for me."

"You could have stopped him. You could have said it was of no value to you. Edgar left his land rather than hold it from a Norman and now if they catch him because of your silly trinket, it will be your fault."

"No, Eldred," his wife put her arm round Goda, "if the girl missed her brooch it was natural for her to say so, besides how could she have known that Edgar would be foolish enough to run back for it?"

"She must have encouraged him."

"I didn't know, I didn't know," Goda wept, clinging to her mother. The often savage resentment of her stepfather frightened her. They were leaving their home and their friends (she forgot how much at first she had welcomed the excitement) simply because he refused to swear what would have been merely lip service to their conquerors. Perhaps if Edgar were trapped inside Exeter, he would be luckier than themselves.

"It will take another hour for the Godwin retainers to embark," Merewin took the smith's great bundle to add to their pile, "the boy is a good runner, he will be here in time."

The field was clearer but the bank was now thick with

people waiting their turn to embark. Most of their burdens were too heavy to carry easily on this slippery winter morning; now and again a man put down his pack after glancing back to see that the Normans were not already on the battlements, and stood there, staring at the ground as if he could not take another step. "They're from the farms and this is the second time they've had to move," it was only after she had spoken that Elfleda realized that she was a fugitive herself.

The bright orange embroidery at the bottom of a curtain sprawled across a sack of beans, a small boy, pretending it was a helmet, balanced a cooking pot on his head, two men carried a barrel past on a board from a trestle table. "Oh, look!" Even Eldred had to laugh. A youth let the handle of his bucket slip and several spoons, a clean shirt and a pot of honey that cracked at once, flew into the mud. The boy put his finger into the honey and licked it, dirt and all. "Serves them right for leaving the place where they were born," the serving woman mumbled.

Men, women, children, there seemed no end to the throng. The youth still knelt in front of them, scooping the honey out of the shattered pot and occasionally spitting out pellets of sticky earth. A man with a bandaged shoulder stumbled against a clod and Eldred sprang forward to help him. "Treachery, nothing but treachery," the fellow recognized the smith, "so you're going too? We could have picked off the Normans one by one as they tried to get through the breach but those old men on the Council were afraid for their lands. They made peace, I didn't."

"When were you wounded?"

"Three days ago at the angle of the East Wall. An arrow came through my shield but its force was almost spent. It will heal in a week or two and then I shall follow the Godwins wherever they settle. But I'd like to burn Exeter and the traitors inside it, even if it is my birthplace."

"Way!" There was a shout along the line and the people crowded back towards the swamps until some of them were up to their knees in thin, watery slime. "What a scarlet!" Elfleda scrambled on top of a pack to get a better view of the great mantle flung back from the man's shoulders, "It must be the head falconer himself." The winter sunlight flashed from the silver studs on his belt, he carried a superb, hooded bird on his leather glove and moved quietly, looking neither to left nor right, as if he were bound for a simple day's hunting in the marshes.

"Way!" A pace or two behind him, men marched in couples, some with hawks, some with sacks. "Look at that cage! They are even taking the young birds," Eldred forgot his anger as he stared in admiration at the procession. He had often wanted to hunt himself but when would a smith have time? There was always the problem of keeping up the fire. "Ah!" Wet and shivering as they were, a roar of admiration rose from the crowd; six boys, the Godwin badge on their coats, passed in front of them, leading the hounds that were the pride of Harold's sons.

Oh, where was Edgar? Goda looked guiltily round but there was not a sign of the youth. He had often said that his great wish was to see the pack. "They keep their coats as burnished as a girl her hair," Elfleda was chattering on, hoping to deflect Eldred's attention from her daughter; one, in particular, was rubbing its tawny back against the dog ward's bright blue cloak as they stopped in front of them for a man to adjust his load.

The shadow of a spear fell on the path, a red plume waved, one of the dogs sniffed at a bush and the boy who was leading it jerked its lead. Goda looked anxiously back towards the city. It had been kind of the Sussex boy to race back and risk his liberty to search for her brooch but in consequence, how angry, how helpless, she felt. "Don't fret," her mother patted her arm, "if he misses us, Edgar knows where the *Seabird* is anchored."

"Way!" The crowd had begun to surge across the path again but an official motioned them back. Eldred could just see the dog ward leading his charges across a narrow plank. He did not want the animals to fall into alien hands but to own the best bred hawks and hounds in England did not necessarily make a man a leader. "Oh, why didn't the Godwins march on Winchester," he muttered angrily to Merewin for the tenth or eleventh time, "they should have taken advantage of a winter surprise as King Harold did in Wales and the West would have remained in our hands." Nobody answered and he wondered if destiny singled out a man to command when he was born or left it, as it seemed at this moment, to chance?

"The housecarls!" The smith pushed forward as far as he dare to watch them pass. They were less well trained than Godric would have desired, he would never have permitted that greasy leather jacket nor the careless slope of some of the axes but their weapons were nicked from combat and they had eighteen days of fighting on the wall behind them. Yes, they could have held the breach. The surrender had come from the men inside the Council Hall. It was a generation that had had no experience of battle and they wanted their firesides and their lands. So it was the ships for the Godwins and their followers, it was this sailing of a winter morning and what the future held for them all, no man could foretell.

There was a pause. The soldiers had to form into a single line to board and two or three boats were already far down the river on their way to the sea. What was Thorkell doing? He had not sent a messenger and the smith's party stood isolated on their hummock as if everybody (but the Normans) had forgotten them. Eldred began to wonder uneasily if they would get away in time. A few men straggled after the housecarls, farmers probably who knew they had lost their fields, some carried shields or had a few metal rings stitched to the shoulders of their coats but they were not properly armed. A figure slipped away from the last row and ran smilingly not to Goda but to her mother. "It was lying under a stool," the silver loop with the dark amber stone set in its circle shone in the middle of his palm, "it is much too beautiful an object to leave to those Norman wolves."

Eldred was the first to thank him. Of course, how stupid of him, the youth had not run back to please a careless girl as he had thought but because he wanted to render a service to his benefactor. "What is it like now inside Exeter? Have the Duke's men entered?"

"I was in such a hurry that all I noticed was the silence, one or two people peeped from their doors but there was nobody in the streets. The watchmen told me at the West Gate that a lot of women and children had gone in supplication to the Duke. They'll learn, as we did in Sussex," he added bitterly. "But if I had not had the luck to see Redwald I might not have got back to you. They were stopping everybody but the Godwin retainers but he made a place for me in their ranks."

The bank was clear at last but rows of heads were watching the path from the side of the boat. "It's the Queen!" Goda pushed her way forward through the few last fugitives grouped round her stepfather. "The Queen!" The word passed from mouth to mouth but the procession that approached them was not like the great assembly that Eldred had seen at Hereford when sword had clashed against shield and a hundred housecarls had roared their loyalty to Earl Harold, nor was it like the feast where from the outer benches where Godric's men had sat, he had looked up to the dais across the jerkins and coats that, poppy red or cornflower blue, had reminded him of a Devon field in summer. The officials who were approaching now, their fur cloaks swinging open to show their gold and silver chains, walked so slowly that they appeared to be deliberately wasting time. "The priests," Elfleda tugged his sleeve, "they're from Queen Gytha's own church. The next services . . ." she could not continue but he knew what she meant, their new rulers would appoint their own men to the poorest parishes and where could the women turn for consolation who had lost their sons and their homes?

Goda recognized her old enemy, the doorkeeper, and here and there a face she knew among the servants. She saw herself standing again in those cold, drafty passages, waiting till they called her. Yet with the fickleness of her age, she wondered if she ought not to throw herself in front of the Queen and beg to rejoin her service? It was so still that her former mistress walked past the little group before she could follow her impulse to run forward and kneel. All she could see were the black robes, the impassive face behind the white band that made her look like a nun and the sorrowful eyes of her daughter, Lady Gunhild, walking a pace behind her mother.

It was a funeral, not a leave-taking; Eldred was aware, as he knelt in homage beside the others, that this was the procession that had been King Harold's due and that the conqueror had denied him. It was a symbol of the names that would disappear, of families now disunited, the slain, and those leaving to die in who knew what foreign earth? The ship and the shingle would continue, they were independent of the land, the hall and the harper would be lost.

There was not even the cry of a gull as the young Godwins, followed by a standard bearer, the last of their company, boarded their waiting ship.

VIII

A man's home was his harbor, like a ship he had to have a port. He rested there, thinking of the shallows and the white curls that warned him of a sunken rock, while he worked out his summer destination, giving due weight to both hazards and rewards. The fields slipped past, Thorkell could hear a swishing among the reeds as the water drove them inland towards the banks, but the port reeve's men had done their job well in October, the channel was clear. He swore that he would not look at his house as he passed it, he would feel a lightening of spirit as they came to the open sea, but the dreams of the past winter overwhelmed him—all those foolish mutterings, "They will give me thane right, after my next voyage," the hope of safety, of a slow, gradual rooting into the land. Lost, all lost, as it had been perhaps from the beginning. What he remembered of his Frisian birthplace was a scoop of sand where he had sheltered from the rain.

Yet he had always been conscious of something, not a lack but a difference, of life, even lives, before memory began, shadowy, half felt impulses vanishing like spray from his finger tips if he lifted a hand to feel the wind. Perhaps because he had been almost born at sea, he had valued the quiet seasons in his garden as if he had been a much older man. He would not look round, he must not look round, if an anchor stuck and had to be cut loose a sailor left it to its fate, perhaps even now the Normans were burning his trees for firewood and spitting against his clean walls. At least he had saved his chest and his movable possessions. Several of his friends had left the previous summer for Flanders. They had foreseen that the Duke would march against the West. He ought to have joined them and it was his own happiness that had betrayed him. Happiness! In spite of his resolution he turned his head as Osmund steered the ship round the last loop of the river but all he could see was his roof, an oak sapling that had seeded itself by the gate and the tip of a fence. The city itself looked exactly as usual because they were too far off to see the breach in the wall at this point.

The wind freshened as they came to the open sea. Thorkell felt himself sway with the ship's roll (how soon a sailor lost his landsman's legs!), it was a miracle that the wind was coming from the right quarter because neither he, nor he supposed any other captain in the fleet, had been out in January before and the challenge began to soften his loss. He had the *Seabird*. He looked up the sail and forward to the carved point of her bow, she had not failed him and, thanks to her, he might save his freedom and some of his wealth. Not one of the Council would have lifted a finger to rescue him although they had bought his cargoes and his wines. "Foreigner," that was all they would have thought although he had grown up on the banks of the Exe. Perhaps it was as well that he had been forced back to the sea once more, his dream of becoming a thane would have been doomed to failure from the start. Only birthright counted with those stay-at-home citizens, nobody had really accepted him except Eldred and that was because the smith had been years on the border, mixing with men from different towns. "Keep well out," he walked over to Osmund who was waiting for him, "even if we are alone, it's safer to be away from the cliffs." Then because he knew that the steersman was longing to ask him the question but would never do so directly, he added, "If the weather holds, let us sail as far as possible before looking for an anchorage, a single ship will have more chance of getting food than the whole fleet."

Now that the first step of their flight was accomplished, Edgar was probably the happiest person aboard. He had got over his seasickness on his previous voyage and each time that the *Seabird* dived into a hollow and rose to a crest again, he knew that he was going towards his rightful destiny; Redwald, on their march towards the river, had promised him a place in his band. He had been one of the few to doubt that Exeter would resist; he lacked the words (though not the feelings) to make those townspeople understand what his villagers had faced. No Norman kept his word, every Norman was hungry for land.

If they had been ready to die rather than surrender, with those thick walls round them and their many axemen, they could have held that breach. He was sorry for his benefactor, few men would have stopped to drag a dirty, starving boy into safety at such a time and fewer still would have given him a sword, but for himself he did not care if he never returned to Wessex, the band would be a substitute for all that he had lost. Meanwhile, as they dipped into the green, racing waves tipped with froth like the feathers on a helmet, he felt like shouting a battle cry as a salute to the future.

"It was kind of you to fetch my brooch." To his amazement Goda had crept out of the shelter they had built for the women, some of the crew had also brought their wives aboard, and was clutching the bulwark at his side. Her cloak almost flew over her head as a gust of wind caught it, she grabbed it with both hands and laughed.

"So you're not sick? Coming from Wessex, I was ill for two days."

"I should be if I stopped behind that old bit of canvas, it smells of fish scales and oil."

"You are brave to leave your city and not be afraid."

"And what did I ever see of Exeter?" When life was upside down she was not going to restrict herself to the "yes" and "no" that her mother had ordered her to use with those who were not members of the household. "I helped in the kitchen and sometimes we went to pick berries from the hedges but always from the same places. The months I spent with the Queen were even worse, she lived in church."

"Your mother is so strict." Nothing would break down

Elfleda's dislike of him although he could not think of any act of his that might have provoked her. "Where I lived, the girls were much freer, we used to go out in groups to the fields, to play or to gather roots." It was true that they had been the village children and that if he had had a sister, she would have been kept like Goda, with the women of the house.

"She minds leaving more than any of us." A strand of hair escaped from the girl's hood and she tucked it hastily inside again, "Her eyes are closed but she is grieving about the house more than being actually sick. I've never been on a ship before and I wanted to look at the water. It's the first time I've seen it from so high up and not moving flatly in to the shingle." Her mother had seldom been willing to take her along the river, she said it was too muddy, and they had gone perhaps twice in a summer to the beach.

"I saw a brooch once with a stone in the center of it as blue as this sea. Perhaps if I have weapon luck with Redwald, I can find one like it as a gift for you."

"You mustn't talk about brooches," Goda clung to the bulwark as they plunged wildly down a wave. Edgar clutched her to keep her on her feet and they both laughed. "But I like the *Seabird*, I have never been so happy in my life."

"You mustn't let your stepfather hear you say that or he will scold you."

"If people are gay, I think he is jealous of them. He minds leaving Exeter because it surrendered, not because he lost his forge."

"It's not the same as losing land," a particular meadow

cut by a little stream flashed across Edgar's memory, he was the heir but strangers ruled his inheritance and he had lost his ancestry, he felt, as well as his fields.

"I'm sorry." Goda was troubled again, as she often was, by not knowing what to say. There were many things she did not understand, such as why Edgar looked suddenly so grim, he had been smiling at her a minute before, and why people talked so much about their birthplace She wanted to see new cities and take the pleasant moments when they came; the past was over and she would face tomorrow when it happened.

"I did not know I had an extra sailor on board," it eased Thorkell's anxiety to see the youngest members of his party acting like truants on a summer day instead of fretting over what they had lost, "I shall have to send you forward with a lantern tonight to keep your watch."

"I like these waves. I never dreamed I should see the shore from the side of a ship."

"But it's a miracle, this wind," Edgar repeated soberly what every man on the *Seabird* had already said. Exeter was famous for the mildness of its winters but the hardiest fisherman put up his boat before the November gales. It would be discourteous to ask the question directly but he wondered where they were bound?

"I hope we can sail as far as West Cornwall before the breeze changes," the Frisian seemed to have read his thoughts, "the Godwins are bound for Ireland in search of more men but that's a voyage none of us can attempt till spring." He would have to find some cargo and the best place for that would be a port on the Welsh coast. "It's three days from Milford to Dublin but it's across the open sea so we shall have to anchor somewhere till the weather is settled."

Cornwall, Wales, Ireland, these were names to Goda. They represented shadows. She wanted to go on watching the gulls diving insolently into the sea and the blue, flecked water behind them. How rich she was! They had lost the great bin of meal to her mother's grief, they had only been able to empty a portion of it into two sacks, but she was going to see places of which she had never heard and have experiences unlike those of any of the neighbors' daughters. "I'll go anywhere," she said with such enthusiasm that Thorkell laughed, such ignorant fearlessness was a relief at such a moment, then Osmund shifted their direction and instinctively he turned his head, it was almost noon but the spires of Exeter were still in sight, shadowy, abandoned, calling to him, the memory of something he had loved that would not let him go.

"Eldred, it's time we sailed." Thorkell looked from the great rock across the bay that was now almost hidden by a clinging, silver mist to the dull, gray shingle at his feet, "We've outstayed our welcome here." The people had rushed down to the beach when they had anchored, hungry for news although only the thane spoke a few words of Saxon and nobody on the *Seabird* knew Cornish, but then the *Gannet*, another Godwin ship, had arrived and what was the fall of a great city compared with the everyday lack of food?

"I can't blame them for being tired of us. Twenty

strangers are too great a burden for this small village."

"They fish the sea instead of tilling the land so naturally the end of winter is the leanest time of the year."

"Some men from the *Gannet* started back yesterday to try to reach their homes."

"They will probably be murdered on their way and if they do get there, what will they find?"

"Norman soldiers." Exeter would have held had Godric been in charge of its defense. "It was treachery and nothing else." Eldred heaved a boulder out with his shoe and kicked it into the waves.

"Careful! Splashing startles the fish." Thorkell had sent two men out in a coracle to see what they could catch. "You will come with me, I suppose."

"It may be foolishness but I can't help feeling Wales will bring me luck." He was anxious about Elfleda. The wife of the thane had taken her into their house but she had not the suppleness of the little sea plant clinging behind him to a mere depression in the rock; her roots had gone too deeply into her native earth and she was homesick. The prouder he was that she had chosen to follow him, the less he seemed able to do for her. "Elfleda never says a word but she misses her kinsfolk. Now Goda seems to thrive on change, she's a different girl."

"She's young! I don't know how long we shall have to wait at Milford because I will not cross the Irish Sea except with a fleet." He would never get over the terror of having been almost captured by a raider and there would be plenty of them out, waiting for single ships. "Once we get to Dublin, your wife can settle down. The sea is rough on weapons and you will have plenty to do as soon as you can start your forge. And Merewin's a good worker, it's fortunate he chose to follow you."

"Yes, he has never grumbled and yet he had hardly been ten miles outside Exeter. He was born on a farm near the North Gate." Eldred glanced instinctively towards the cliffs on his right, they stretched towards what the natives called the corner of the world. "Think what it must mean for him! It takes conquest or plague to force such a man to leave his birthplace."

"He has no rights anywhere else." He, himself, would have to begin over again, Thorkell knew, there would be choices to make, the giving of gifts that now he could hardly afford to the right chiefs, and waiting, waiting, perhaps for whole seasons when his endurance was already thinner than the skeleton of that year-old leaf before him, half buried in sand. "It's the weather, I suppose, I feel as sleepy here in the morning as when I go to bed at night."

"None of us slept much during the siege." Eldred tried to keep the memory of those eighteen days out of his head, then he had been a prosperous smith and now he was a fugitive, but isolated incidents from that time kept coming back to torment him. "It's different here, we should be starting to plow but these people seem to belong to the sea."

"Yes, they fish where even my men are afraid to go. The salt in the spray burns their crops except in a few sheltered hollows, so they find their riches on the sands, driftwood, shell fish, sometimes a cask washed up from a wreck."

"It's the language as well." There had been the same problem on the border but there Eldred had had the power of his housecarl's rank and had expected the market women to learn something of Saxon. It was difficult now for Elfleda; she could never ask a question about where she might cook or how she could help.

"It's easier for us. We know how a man handles his oar and what he calls it does not matter." Thorkell got up a little stiffly from the edge of hard rock where he had been sitting and looked straight out across the water. The uncertainty and the scarcity of food would soon lead to a brawl and deeply as he was in sympathy with his fellow exiles, he was a seaman and knew how harshly and meagerly these fisher folk lived. "Make your preparations," the mist that he was staring at was beginning to clear, "I've never sailed in the black season before but once the wind is right, we start for Milford."

There was no need to get out the great oars as long as the wind filled the sail. Thorkell's men knew, although he had not warned the passengers, that this was the most dangerous part of their journey. The only time that he had rounded the cape before had been in June. Friends of his, experienced captains, refused to risk a passage by the uttermost edge of England and thus the profitable Irish trade was almost entirely in northern hands. Today the weather was with them, they were rolling, of course, but it was a steady motion as long as they were under the shelter of the cliffs and if it held, they ought to reach Milford in a couple of days. They had left at the first light and as the sun rose they could see patches of dead bracken and bare brambles on the hills, all a dingy brown; what color there was, was in the sea. The dangers, Thorkell knew, were in his mind, at least until they reached the point where the ship must turn. He dreamed he was sitting in his room, watching the firelight flicker on the polished chest that now stood, tied up in canvas, under some bales at the stern, and heard his voice muttering again, "Thane's right, after the next voyage." Was that a figure of himself he saw in a fur cloak with a gold chain round the neck and a much heavier build? Or a boy watching a swift and narrow ship racing the fog to board them before they disappeared? Or simply a place full of sunlight and people calling to each other in a tongue he had never heard while they splashed water over blazing, white cobblestones? Past or future, reality or dream, he looked up into a dark, gray sky where two seagulls were waiting to swoop down on the same bit of fish that Osmund was preparing to toss into the water and one of his uncle's rules (it must be the first time for years he had remembered it) echoed in his ears until he almost said it aloud. "Never forget your inheritance." If his uncle had died from a fever in a hut instead of on some sandy bar, it did not alter the meaning. His fears cracked and a feeling of exhilaration replaced them to his astonishment. "It would be in the most dangerous part of the coast," he muttered almost angrily. This was his kingdom, not Exeter, not the slow winding river nor the hall where he had bowed in deference before the councilors. He looked from the top of the mast to where the waves stretched themselves, lifting the ship up till the foam flaked it and then letting it slide again, through gray, blue and scrambling green, into the eternal pattern of hills and valleys. Here he would never be "a foreigner." If he studied the moods and wishes of the ocean, he would be its comrade although never its master, but it had taken a siege and what seemed disinheritance to make him understand. This was the scald's voyage between life and death that they sang of in the hall. Perhaps it was the first time in a century that a ship had passed this way during the winter. Now they were in the sight of the great rocks that were the limit of the world to those Saxons who knew of them and the waves reached shorewards, leaping, climbing, chasing each other like puppies, to surge seaward again whenever they touched the granite of the pinnacles they could not undermine.

Osmund looked grim, many of the sailors had turned their heads to watch the calmer water on their left but Thorkell could not keep his eyes away from the headland and the gulls. No Norman yet had set foot on those moors, no crops would grow in that windswept land. There was grass, heather, any plant that could clutch the earth; the only danger those cliffs had to fear was the sea.

It was almost dark when the *Seabird* came, two days later, in sight of Milford harbor. Thorkell had ordered out the oars, they rose and dipped in the way that Eldred so admired, like the axe swings of Godric's practice. Hill followed low hill, soft and green, his border country again and looking up at the red in the western sky because it was almost sunset, he could not keep himself from thinking that a pennant was out to welcome him back. They did not stop in the main harbor but rowed along an arm of the sea to the front of a small village and as they heaved the anchor over with a splash, two or three coracles came swiftly over from the beach to greet them.

Spring! Yet what could spring, the season of renewal, be to them here? Elfleda looked helplessly at the slime beyond the open door. It was full of fish bones that people spat out as they passed. She had already washed the threshold once that morning but it was marked by muddy footprints and the spine of a distorted leaf stared at her from a crack. The sun was out, this was the month when she would have gone daily to the meadows to collect the new greens and cut young bracken to freshen the winter rushes on her floor. Now she did not know what they would do when it came to prepare the syrups that she needed during the year. Eldred had forbidden her to leave the place without him, "They say the Welsh are friendly but you are not to wander alone," and she had already noticed that none of the women went up into the hills. They bought the sedges for their salves in the market although she, herself, would not have touched them; they had been handled by too many to be fresh enough to use.

It was hard to understand how life could have changed so much in a matter of two months. An earthwork seemed to have risen between Exeter and here. She had known unhappiness before, especially during the last anxious months of Uhtred's life when he had drunk too much and exchanged good land for water-logged fields, and perhaps that had been the moment when she had begun to isolate herself from all her neighbors except Mildburh. It had been possible to accept her cousin's sympathy because Mildburh had never referred to the matter but had found excuses to spend more days outside the city than were necessary, to get her away from her father's fury and the general gossip. Yet angry as she had often been with Uhtred (she was glad now that she had so seldom shown it), he had been gay, kind when she had least expected it, and how he had made them laugh when he had come back from the market, bringing her a ribbon when she had needed a broom, with some story of an old peasant getting the better of his lord or perhaps a new song! Goda was almost too like her father, impulsive, so careless and yet with a warm heart. Here in this smoke filled room for which Eldred had bartered a good spade so that she could be at least alone, she could not keep her daughter by her side. Goda fetched water and ran errands, mixing with the neighbors and listening to their gossip, it was against her feelings as to what was seemly but how could she expect the girl to sit hour after hour in this hut, looking out, not at the orchards of Exeter but at a lane of evil smelling slime?

Eldred was different. He had turned into a person she had never previously known, talking with everyone, joking about his housecarl days, that word "Hereford" was constantly on his lips, looking for dry twigs and branches, not for a forge but for her own fire. He had even established a truce with Goda, "Let the girl make friends wherever she can," but what they were going to do, where they would settle, the burning question for her of when they would have a home again, seemed never to enter his mind. The Queen was living on Flatholm, many of the merchants had already sailed for Flanders, there was talk of Dublin and even of the North. Wherever they went it would mean new customs and a strange language. She put her hands over her face and tried to imagine the boughs of Mildburh's apple tree coming into flower. Oh, how dirty it was here and lonely! She seemed incapable of linking up with the wives of the other exiles, most of them had given up any pretense of cleanliness and were as dusty and flea ridden as their hosts. What she wanted was to hang her own freshly washed linen on the line again while the cries of her native city, "Rushes, ellenwort, a handful of bothen," echoed (as they should do) in her ears.

"Dublin is your best choice." Those white markings might be a chart, the Frisian thought, turning over a gray pebble with his toe. Yet there would be nothing to follow if he picked it up, the lines led only into the shingle.

"But their smiths are famous. Nothing I can forge can match their work."

"Nor would they let you try. But you have the right to land as a retainer of the Godwins and they have enough weapons to keep you busy all summer."

"I feel at home here." Whenever Eldred looked at the huts climbing the hill in an irregular line, he did not see the inside filth nor the muddy tracks that so disturbed Elfleda but the free wilderness of bramble covered moor. It seemed to belong to him more than his own birthplace, although this was a thought that he must naturally conceal.

"And how would you live?" Thorkell sympathized with his friend, he had never known him so carefree and so happy but practical difficulties had to be faced. "If they would let you set up a forge, I should say find a house and settle down but there are two smiths now, within five miles of each other, and both complain they have not enough work."

"Neither of them knows as much about their craft as I do."

"Judging by the way one of them mended a spoke of my anchor, I agree, but they were born here, you were not, and no headman is going to turn out a fellow villager to admit a stranger. No, if you insist on staying you will have to turn laborer and find a farmer who will hire you."

"Give me time to think it over."

"You can have till tomorrow morning but no longer. This time I want to sail in the middle of the fleet. There will be raiders from all directions waiting for the boat that slips behind or has the misfortune to break a mast. Remember, if you reach Ireland and do not like it, you can always leave. The Godwins say that if they get enough men, they will attack the Normans in the summer." It was wiser not to add that he was doubtful of their success. There would be too many masters in whatever force they collected. He was only anxious about his friend. Eldred had already bartered away more of his sparse possessions than was wise but at Dublin, especially if more men joined the army, a smith would find plenty of work. "Tell me, at the latest, by this hour tomorrow. Directly the wind shifts in the right direction we shall sail." He strolled off to where Osmund was working busily over a splintered cask, at such a moment it was better for Eldred to work out his future by himself.

Loyalty alone required him to remain with the Godwins, the smith was as aware of this as of his wife's unhappiness in this lonely village. Many of their fellow fugitives were living in mere hovels scraped out of the hillside, and they had owned rich farms as late as Christmas, so as to keep enough to buy a place on deck when the fleet left. Dublin to them was a place of opportunity and gold. For himself, it would be a return to the life he hated and from which he had twice been freed; once when he had run away to join the housecarls and now by his flight from Exeter to these moors. He supposed it was a memory of youth but he already had roots in this village. Sometimes he met Welshmen on the paths and, foolish as this was, he waited for a man, some day, to sing out his name. Kynan! Would he recognize the boy if they should meet? Boy! Kynan must be a man now with his own cows and hearth. Yes, they were both years older but the eyes, the quick, upturned curve of the mouth, the black, shaggy hair, would not have changed. It was foolish, even as a thought, because Kynan's Wales was a week's journey from here on the best pony that a man could buy. Foolish . . . yet a man would give up life itself more easily than his dreams.

Eldred walked slowly up to the market place. Some old women and a youth or two were sitting on a low wall behind bales of fodder and the jars of heather scented honey that the exiles could not afford to buy. He could not get the conviction out of his mind that Kynan or some messenger who had seen him would be there. He did not want to go to Ireland, a foreboding clung about the name for him, his father had spoken of its smiths, it was a land at the end of the world. It was here that he was at home, and he hurried on, past the booths, up towards the wilder country where the villagers never went except in groups, higher and higher till he came to the brambles, a few late ones were still in flower, scrambling between bush and bush as he had done so often in the past, thinking of Godric, of the pallid fern in the cave where Kynan had sheltered him, and the shadows of the long march back to his companions. He was not lost, looking back in the direction of Exeter (strange to think of Exeter now being east!), he could see the *Seabird* at anchor close to the shore. It was the scent, the murmuring of the grasses and the bracken, the slithering away of a mouse, the wide sky, this moment when, as if born again, he stood up on the hillside as a youth, but knowing now what it meant to be twenty and full of power, that was his here and nowhere else. If he remained the spell (could it be anything else?) would be upon him and age would be as far away as he was now from his birth. If he sailed with the fleet, and he did not hold the shivering that came over him as foolishness, he entered a fog his eyes could not pierce.

"Tell me tomorrow at latest." Those small dots he could see below the *Seabird* must be the crew cleaning out the ship. If he were alone, he would work happily as a shepherd, forgetting the dwelling that had once been his and his craft. But Elfleda? He saw her face as he had seen it that morning, so unhappy, so afraid. She had followed him instead of remaining with her kinsfolk and he had sworn to protect her. Sadly, his head bent towards the ground so that he could not see the outline of the hills rising sharply against the clear blue sky, he walked back to the port.

IX

The sea moved in slow, silver circles up to the shingle, the landscape beyond it was a row of low hills. A number of ships were already pulled up on the shore and the black dots beyond them were sailors, carrying stores up to the camp. "King Diarmid has welcomed the exiles," Thorkell pointed to a small craft that was rowing towards them, "but the place is full of Northmen who have settled here, that is not a native boat."

There was a little wind as the *Seabird* moved gently through the mild, damp air. Too gently, Elfleda thought, she wanted their arrival to be over. What fate waited for them on that sandy beach that for the moment was a crescent immediately in front of them? Dublin? The name was beginning to have a meaning for her as the place where she might spend the rest of her life. She looked down at the water, trying to foresee (but this was impossible) what the future would hold, but all that was apparent was a hollow wave and a white eddy of spray. She was frightened as she had never been during the siege but then she had had the pride of her birthplace to sustain her. Now she was shivering with the fearful anxiety that had plagued her during Uhtred's last years when she had never known if he might not be stabbed in a brawl or sell more of her fields over her head? She need not have worried, her house had gone all the same, and much as she loved Mildburh she did not trust her cousin. Frain, if he sold the place, would keep the proceeds for himself under the pretext that he did not know where his kinswoman was, although they had tried to send a message back to him from Wales. She had suffered a great deal in the smoky, Milford hut but as she looked towards the almost black edges of the mountains, exile suddenly became the true center of life and not a temporary discomfort to be endured for a couple of months. What other ending could there be? The moment that her feet touched dry land, she would reach the place where she would probably die. She looked down in panic at the now familiar planks of the ship and then up at Thorkell's reassuring face. Oh, if a person could turn back the sequences of life and make a different choice! If only her will had been stronger and she had told her father that she would not marry Uhtred, she might have been able later to break down Eldred's reticence and reconcile him with his city. Then they might still have their home. Or she might have loved her house less and Eldred more and then this wandering would not seem so terrible. He would have been loyal to the Godwins, that she knew, but she might have been less jealous of their hold over him. Yet who could help their passions? At best she could stifle hers but it came back at the end to the simply primitive facts of exile, hunger and death. "Goda!" She needed a human touch to console her at this moment but her daughter was standing at the bow, chattering happily to the Saxon youth. He was landless and no fit companion for her but people persisted in saying, "Isn't it lucky in these times to find two young people so happy?"

"I think you will like it here," Thorkell said softly as if he had guessed her feelings, "King Diarmid, they say, is treating the young Godwins as if they were his own sons."

"I have felt safe on your ship." It was not quite true but Elfleda believed it at this moment. The *Seabird* was familiar, she had often passed it at anchor, walking with Eldred on feast days along the winding banks of the Exe. Besides, now that she was accustomed to her own corner at the stern, she feared the search for another dwelling so much that only force, she felt, would get her into a coracle. Mildburh! Had her friend remembered to collect the spinning wheel and had Frain sold the house? Her heart was with her friends but it was her duty to stay with Eldred, and like a burr caught in a thick, woolen coat, she could not dislodge herself from her fate.

"It's a pleasant spot," as Merewin handed his master a broken ring that he had just cut from the shoulder of a heavy, leather coat, Eldred noticed that the old man was moving more briskly than he had done for years. "The water is good and the people are kind. Last week, when we had the holiday they took me to a farm in the hills and, if it had not been for the language, I might have been back in my own village."

"Then you're not homesick?" Eldred threw a log recklessly on the fire, it was easier to get wood here than in Devon.

"No, I should like to tell my friends about rounding the edge of the world, especially the swineherd that came to the market, do you remember he always wore a green hood with a rent in it, but otherwise I am happy here. What does it matter where a man lives if he can work at his trade?" He wiped his fingers on a greasy apron and detached a second ring, "This one has had a cut across it sometime, it is not worth mending."

"Yes," Eldred nodded, for the first time in his life he was content simply to attend to his forge. It was Elfleda now who lived for the victory that would permit her to return to her home, though she never let a word about it pass her lips. He had not even considered asking for a place on the fleet that was about to invade England.

"We are old, Merewin," he muttered and then, as if to contradict himself, he struck such a blow on the anvil that sparks flew, arrow-wise, through the air.

A man passed, whistling one of the battle songs, some soldiers were dragging casks down to the shore. Of course he would be envious when the ships sailed but there were too many captains and each would follow his own path. At least he would still have the Frisian's company. Thorkell asserted that the *Seabird* was unfit to leave although the smith suspected it was merely an excuse to remain longer in Ireland. It was the little details that came back to him as he hammered out the rings (they had promised to finish the man's coat by dusk), it was not the spires of the churches or the wains full of corn, but a dead yellow leaf the shape of a lance that had caught his eye the day he had found Edgar or a gay blue head cloth hanging out on Elfleda's line. "We lost," he thought, "but how?" The housecarls had been as brave as the Duke's men but a lethargy had fallen upon England. Nobody had been able to choose between the essential and their familiar customs. Too many soldiers had been killed at Stamford, the hurried march south had not given the survivors time to sleep off their fatigue, the strangeness of the mine had quenched resistance at Exeter. These were facts, the real conflict was in the mind. The Normans, much as he hated them, had had one purpose in view and it was conquest. All that he valued most would pass away and would never return. Conquest! Even their language would change, the words that beat in his ears with the thundering roll of the waves, were fugitives like himself and would alter or disappear.

Those who loved their land were least loved by it. Godric had trained him to recognize, if he could not accept, defeat.

The exiles were quartered in one part of the camp while the Northmen lived on the other side of the settlement. It was idle to pretend that there was no quarreling between them but their leaders tried to keep them from fighting each other. "Stay inside your tents, we cannot afford to lose a single soldier," Redwald shouted at his men every morning. The ships were due to leave in less than a week, a battle fleet this time without a fugitive aboard.

"May I have a word with you, Master Thorkell?" Edgar stood with the sun shining so directly onto his freckled face that he blinked.

"Come in, come in," the merchant was astonished to see the youth and supposed he brought some message from the smith.

"It's a question about myself." Edgar fingered his knife as if he did not know what to do with his hands nor how to begin his query and he looked up at Thorkell with the bewildered air of a hound shut up in the kennels while the rest of the pack was loosed to hunt in the fields.

"Why should you not come to me after our voyage together?" Thorkell wondered if Edgar knew what a feat it was to have rounded that cape in January, as he shouted to his old cook who had survived the journey with many grumbles, to bring in ale and a loaf of bread. "Well, what is it?" he asked as kindly as possible. He wondered what was tormenting the youth who seemed to have lost his voice and perhaps his wits.

"I expected to stay with Redwald," again Edgar hesitated and this surprised the Frisian even more because the youth generally babbled the first words that came into his head. "I was so proud of being in his band."

"Have you quarreled with someone?" You could not keep men who had lost their halls and their richer northern neighbors together without trouble. Perhaps Edgar needed money because of some feud?

"I will fight the Normans if I am one against five. They killed my father and robbed me of my land." He repeated the sentence that his comrades heard at least six times a day.

"Well, the fleet is sailing with a whole army next week."

"Yes, but . . ."

"You do not want to plunder and fire an English village." From the relief on the youth's face, Thorkell knew that he had found the right answer.

"The Godwins and Redwald want it no more than I do but it is the Northmen's price. They insist upon attacking the 'soft part' first and say if they harry Devon, the Normans will have no supplies."

"They may go short of corn but it will drive the farmers into the Duke's ranks."

"How can I burn down a barn and slay its owner when he speaks my language?" Edgar seemed as puzzled as he was shocked. "I've worked on my own fields, I know how hard and cold it is to plow and the hunger that comes if a storm destroys the crops."

"If they antagonize the peasants they will lose England."

"Yes," Edgar looked grimly down at the floor and left his ale untasted in front of him.

"It's hard for the Godwins. Their forces are too small for them to attack alone but the West to their allies is merely a place to loot. Yet if the price of attacking Exeter is to waste the countryside, the citizens will welcome the Duke as their rescuer."

"I said this to Redwald last night and he told me to be silent."

"And you want to know what to do?"

"I cannot go back and accept Master Eldred's charity. Half the soldiers are promising to pay him only on their return and he has barely enough for himself. I wondered . . ." he hesitated again because it was a great favor to ask, "if there would be a place for me on your ship?"

"No, Edgar," the merchant looked him up and down from his fair hair to his ox hide shoes, "a sailor is born to his calling and one day, I hope, you will win back some land. I bartered some wool the other day for timber and if Redwald will release you, I will send you with my men to fetch it as an additional guard. Then after the fleet has left, I will speak to my friend Osbern. He is from the North but he thinks the attack is a foolish venture. If you take service with him, you will have to go with him to his home but you will not have to take up arms against your own people."

"If there is anything I can do for you," Edgar looked up with such gratitude that Thorkell laughed. "No, do not thank me, it is stupid to get killed in an unplanned foray and what chance is there that a force bent on plunder and some headstrong exiles can win back England? All they have is hope and a few fine words. But keep your mouth shut till I have got you out of this camp."

It was a soft land, turned inwards on itself and moving, not as in Devon from bay to bay but from lake to lake or, where there was no water, low, green hills. Thorkell was thankful that he had decided to take a holiday and accompany Edgar and his men to get the new spar for his ship. These Irish trees grew straight. It was safer to be away from Dublin when the fleet sailed, they had grumbled at him for not joining it. He was almost used now to the loss of Exeter, could even see it as a blessing because the April winds would call him back to the *Seabird* till he died. He seemed to be standing apart from the exiles simply because he still had a country, his boat. Yet how much longer would it be before another raider surprised him and sold him into slavery or he was drowned on the inevitable shoal? This land, so green and gray and silver under the hooves of the ponies, was not a place where he could settle, he must find a city that would not remind him of the Exe. His uncle had made him learn enough figures so that he could repeat the numbers that a port reeve scrawled on a cask. He had once had a friend in Flanders who had spoken of a sailor who could actually read. "A Greek, you know, they treat their captains in the south as if they were Earls." It was not the monkish foolishness that his uncle ·had said; he knew there would be less danger if he could write down the rocks and eddies he noticed along the coast. Suppose some knowledge, some new experience, filled the emptiness that the loss of his home had left in his mind? "I have the *Seabird*," he muttered, "I have my ship." It was hard to think of perils on this ride when the grass was as full of flowers as a curtain of colored stitches and the sky was a wide arch. South? It was a long distance away past headlands he did not know. "What did you say?" Edgar asked so he must have said something aloud. "Oh, nothing, I was trying to remember the Irish word for grass, you have been a farmer, you must envy them their meadows."

X

Oh, these rats!" Eldred turned to hit a scurrying form with a billet of wood. "It's always a bad sign when they come into a house, they flood the place with fleas." Not that he could call this hut a house, it was simply a shelter built from stakes and blocks of peat. It was a continual grief to him that he had not been able to provide Elfleda with a better dwelling although it was identical with the other places in the camp but work was scarce. The Northmen with their plunder went to the Irish smiths and all he got was some broken tool to mend or a blunt knife to sharpen. "At least, Thorkell, the rain has stopped. I suppose you will soon be leaving us? Have you decided yet where you will go?"

"Flanders or France, I suppose, there is not much choice." He did not want to speak of a fellow captain's suggestion. "Come south with me in the summer, I will show you my chart. It's dangerous, yes, but once there each city is richer than its neighbor and the winters are short." If he accepted the offer he would never see his friends again because he would not return to the ever more unsettled North.

"If only the Godwins . . ."

"Make up your mind, Eldred, that their cause is lost. They are too weak to invade the West alone and their Northern friends think only of plunder."

"Yet what are we to do?" They were all getting poorer every day and they could not even leave the boundary of their camp. "If it had not been for Elfleda, it would have been better to have stayed in Wales, it was a more familiar landscape." His wife had made friends here with some of the other women but always with those who, like herself, could not get over their homesickness.

"I can take you back there if you wish. Wherever I go, I shall put into Milford first for water and provisions."

The problems would be the same as they were here and at least for the moment the Godwins would not let their old retainers starve. Thorkell looked round him at the figures sitting silently on the littered dirty grass and longed almost savagely for the sea.

"Men live, men die." Eldred was not thinking about the meaning of the words, he was wishing that somebody would ask him to make a new dagger.

"It's the idleness that is so hard, we remember too much."

"And the rats, there's another one, I'm always afraid they will get at our sack of meal."

"You need not decide today, it will be a month before

I leave." It was a matter of endurance, of not letting memory conquer, perhaps it was easier for him because, unlike Eldred, he had never had a country. "We sailed in January when no ship had put to sea before, something will happen, in a year's time we shall forget this dreary beach."

"The beach perhaps but not the rats" and Eldred killed another one that was slithering through a hole in the peat.

One morning it was April, the winter was over and the usual restlessness was stirring in men's hearts. Then, and it was only a matter of hours, people lay choking for breath and often dying, in almost every hut. "It's the plague," an old man muttered but his neighbor checked him, "Silence, you fool, it's the spring sickness and it doesn't affect the healthy. Shut your mouth or the Irish will stop away and how shall we get our food?"

"It's because of our sins."

"Our boasting, our lying."

"I vow, I vow I will go on pilgrimage."

"And who will give you the shoes, grandmother, or the food?" Even the old man who had been scolded, laughed.

"This is an evil place, we should never have landed here, we are being punished for our misdeeds."

"The Normans did worse and nothing happened to them. If we deserve punishment, it's because we sit around the fire and talk about the past instead of sailing home to wrest back our inheritance."

The buds came out on the brambles, the sky, the butterflies and the early flowers were the same light blue but in all the beauty of the growing year one hut after the other grew empty.

"Edgar!" The youth looked up in surprise when he heard Goda's voice, it was not customary for women to enter the soldiers' part of the camp.

"Edgar! I told the watchman I had to find my kinsman. My stepfather is ill and nothing we do helps him."

"Ill! Since when?"

"Since yesterday at noon. By night time he was wandering in his mind."

"If it's the plague, there is nothing to do but pray." A sword cut was a sword cut, as Edgar often said, and if a man was hit it was due to his own carelessness but plague . . . that was an evil outside human experience, it could paralyze both sword arm and will and he knew no honest way in which to fight it. Some of his comrades said that it came from a wickedness that lurked into a person's thoughts while he slept but he preferred Redwald's view that it was a blow from fate or whatever it was that held a man's destiny in its grasp. He was afraid, he twisted his cloak in his hands to keep them from shaking but he must go to Eldred, without the smith's help he would neither be here nor alive. "I heard a trader say yesterday he had brought some drug from a foreign port and that even six drops will revive a man who is at lip touch with death. If I can find him, I'll give him my extra dagger for a dose of it."

"Oh, Edgar, if you would!" She did not say for her

mother's sake because she knew how the young man felt about Elfleda. Yet to offer a weapon was a great sacrifice and she was grateful.

"But Goda, go to some neighbor yourself." He looked anxiously at the girl's healthily red cheeks. "It's a ravenous sickness, if it claims one victim, there is often a second . . . ," he checked himself before saying a third.

"My mother is sending me away. She told me to find you and then I am to go to Aethelflaed. She says, and it's true, there's no place for two women and a sick man in our small hut."

Eldred's mind cleared gradually although he could not move his limbs but the wavering, hardly conscious thoughts of the last days had vanished. He could distinguish the bowl on the floor from the rushes on which it stood and the outline of Elfleda's head, she was sitting beside the fire. He was surprised how much existed inside him, memories crossed his mind and were lost in a mist before he could clearly recall them, he tried to remember the sun's heat on a bare neck instead of the damp smell of the moldy wall at his elbow or the raw scents of a fern covered slope. A weight was pressing on his chest, it was not quite heavy enough to stop his breathing but he wished it would cease. Death was only a welcome haven to which he had been advancing all his life. Life? It had built once to a climax of sun, heather and happiness, now it had fallen to a choking fear that this agony would never end. The shield line, the forays, and the walls, those who had fallen when the arrows hit them, had had an easier end than this.

Elfleda stirred. She took the pail and went out to the water butt a few paces beyond their dwelling. Eldred's eyes were closed and she supposed him to be asleep. It was almost sunset, she looked up at the green, mocking sky with flags of scarlet blowing across it and prayed her husband would not have to endure another night, not recognizing her and muttering constantly about a wood in Wales.

They had left their birthplace and this was the answer. A fine, a few words of homage, and they could have stayed in their home. She was loyal to the Godwins, she would never have befriended a Norman but fate was fate. Eldred could not have compromised, she knew, yet sometimes (the thought came back in spite of many resolutions) she wondered what he had gained from these extra years of life? There had been days when he had been gayer than he had ever been at Exeter and others when he had seemed to draw back like an animal into its hole. Were all individuals isolated, like the rocks that she had seen from the ship? They had seemed exactly alike to her yet Thorkell said each stone had a different shape, was bare or had a deeper stain of weed or a ledge that suited the gulls.

Sunset ("They go with the setting of the sun"), she turned back in a panic with her pail only half full lest he slip away while she was absent. She promised herself (as if she could control the matter!) that if he lived past midnight he would recover. "Eldred!" She thought she saw some recognition in his eyes but she was not sure. He was jerking, struggling, memory went with movement, with the pulling that had happened once, the gasping. "Leave the arrow." He wanted to speak, to obliterate the humiliation of the crippled arm, the flight, the loss, to go back to that clearing and die at the height of his strength. "Leave . . . the . . . arrow" but how could Elfleda understand the distorted sounds when she was trying to help him breathe? She was bending over him, wondering what he wanted, when his struggles ceased.

"I wish I had been in time." Thorkell looked sadly down at the form that was now covered by a sheepskin rug. He had been at the shore checking ropes aboard the *Seabird* when the messenger had reached him.

"He wanted to tell me something," Elfleda felt ashamed that all she wanted to do was sleep, "but I could not understand him. The last word sounded like 'arrow.'"

"He might have been remembering his years in Wales."

"Or the walls of Exeter."

"It is merciful. Those who recover from the sickness usually die in a season or two and he would have hated to linger on as a shivering old man." A sudden memory came back of Eldred on the bâttlements, "I used to forget the cold when he walked down with his cloak swinging and a sword at his side to see us on our night watch."

Happiness? Destiny? They gave so much at one moment to snatch it away at the next. Elfleda had wanted to speak of this to her husband but he had never been a man of many words. Now it was too late. How could she say to the body stretched so stiffly on the rushes, "If you could have answered in your mind and not with your lips, if you had stayed beside your forge and never gone where there were Normans, we should still be living in our home and you would have died among your friends." Yet even as the thought came to her she knew that such a person could never have been Eldred and she said aloud, "Whatever he was, Thorkell, he was loyal, loyal to the Godwins and to us."

XI

It's your life, Goda, as well as mine."

"But my mother says . . ."

"She can come with us, I have offered her a home."
There would never be any affection between Dame Elfleda and himself but if her presence was the girl's marriage price, he would put up with her.

"She still believes we can return to Exeter."

The thin, crumpled waves were driving into the ledges
of sand with the force of a flight of arrows. Edgar wondered idly if they came from the Welsh coast? Of course
not, it was too far away. Fate was fate, he thought of
his own lost lands with anger but he could not give himself up to what seemed to him the stupidity of Dame
Elfleda's grief. To fret as she did about her birthplace
would bring nobody good fortune and he believed in
fortune. What else had brought Eldred to him among
those icy, dreary woods? "We were meant for each

other," he was thinking about Eldred as he took her hand, forgetting, as most of them did, that the smith was not her father.

"I know." All Goda saw was that morning on the *Seabird* when the first waves had broken over the bow and the city had receded into a gray blur of spires. They had faced the sea and an unknown future together and she had been happier than ever before in her life. Yet a daughter was told to obey her parents from the instant she could walk and her mother seemed helpless and somehow old since her stepfather had been buried. "Oh, Edgar, how can I sail and leave my mother here? I should never see her again." Nor know, she thought, how she died.

"Think of me, Goda, if not of yourself. I have offered to take your mother with us, I have asked her for no dowry, if she will not go, be brave, what will your life be here?" No other man in the camp would have made a similar offer, he would soon become a laughing-stock to his companions if the girl remained so obstinate, and that would be unendurable.

"Perhaps next year . . ."

"No, Goda, this is something you have to face. I have sworn myself Osbern's man, I shall sit at his board, in a year or two he may give me a little land. You cannot sacrifice yourself to your mother's wishes."

"Give me till tomorrow, Edgar, just till tomorrow."

"I will be here tomorrow at the same time but unless you agree to follow me then, we shall not meet again." She had waited a whole week to see him and now as she looked into his angry eyes and watched him turn and stride away across the fields, her mother's loneliness, the unknown northern wilderness that might forever be her home, whirled in such a tumult inside her head that she wished she herself had caught the plague and died of it.

"Elfleda!"

What was the Frisian doing in this part of the camp and why was he wearing his blue, embroidered shirt on a weekday? The last sword that Eldred had ever made was at his side. "Come in, it was so damp I lit a fire."

"I want to talk to you for a little." He sat down on the stool that she brought him and stared at the blaze as if he did not know how to begin.

"You are leaving, I suppose, and have come to say goodbye." Elfleda picked up several bits of wood one after the other before she found one dry enough to throw on the hearth.

Thorkell was still silent, he seemed to be watching a small twig that first smoldered and then burst suddenly into a brief flame. "Sometimes a stranger sees a problem more clearly than the person it concerns," he pushed his cloak aside as if the cold, damp room were too warm.

"If you mean Goda, she was always willful. The decision now is in her own hands."

"There is something more important than your daughter's marriage," he looked down at his blade as if, thinking of sword play, he would find the words he wanted. "No, no beer," he shook his head as she got up to fetch a jug, "I have to be at the Council in an hour."

"When are you leaving?" The final link with her former life was about to be broken and she felt hopeless and so alone.

"You have moved very little about the camp and that was natural during your time of mourning but even so, you must have heard some rumors."

"Rumors of what?" She was genuinely surprised.

"At first they liked us."

"Yes, an old woman gave me a load of sticks soon after we landed and would take no payment."

"King Diarmid, as they say, is 'gentle to strangers' and when it was a question of some exiles, even if they formed an army, spending a winter here before sailing to retake their lands, it was a matter the Irish could accept. But the Godwins failed last year and the Northmen who joined them have treated the native inhabitants as if they were serfs."

"I have heard stories but I never took much notice of them." Why should she listen when Eldred was dead and Goda such an anxiety to her?

"We have outstayed our welcome. Suppose men burst into this hut some night and carried you and your daughter away as slaves?"

"The King would prevent it. He likes the Godwins."

"That is the danger. They say he favors them more than his own people. Be wise, Elfleda, let the young people go. Osbern will be a good lord to them both."

So it was only another talk to break down her resistance, and she shrugged her shoulders, "They will do what they like. I am the last person who can stop them."

"Let them go with your blessing, Elfleda, it's a long journey."

"The youth has no character."

"He will never be an Eldred but that is better in these times. It won't be easy in the North at first but I think they will be happy."

"Goda is all I have and Merewin has found another master."

"Let them go. You hate me for urging this but it is inevitable."

"While I stay here as, I think you said, a slave." She had brought Goda up, she had often saved her from Eldred's anger and persuaded herself that she still loved the memory of the girl's own father although Goda's obsession with the young Saxon reminded her of Uhtred in his reckless moods. Now she was to be left in this dirty and lawless camp, alone and without kinsfolk.

"No, Elfleda, you must go back to Exeter." Seeing the happiness that she could not keep out of her face, Thorkell knew that he had won his battle.

"To be thrown out as soon as I got to the gates."

"Let Goda leave. It's the girl's destiny. There is just time for them to marry before Osbern sails. I was talking to a captain who anchored yesterday and he says that many women have gone back to the city and were admitted without fines."

Did she want to go back without Goda, without Eldred, full of the beaten, baffled longings of an exile without a home?

"I know I shall never see Exeter again," Thorkell tried to keep his voice as flat and calm as possible, "but there is little trade to be done here and I am sailing in the

Seabird for Wales. Come with me and I will find a passage there for you to return to your home."

"No!" Her house, the old life, were wiped as blank as the beach, where they threw the rubbish, after a storm.

"We have both lost, Elfleda," he did not know his eventual destination but it would be somewhere outside England, "make your preparations, Eldred would have wanted you to follow my advice."

The sun had been out some hours. A succession of coracles bobbed on top of the waves, sank into hollows and emerged on the crest of the water again, taking bales, bundles and people out to the *Spray*. Elfleda felt so empty of feeling that looking at Goda, she was sitting on an empty box beside her, the girl seemed already a stranger.

"Oh, why won't you come with us, Mother?"

"It is better as Thorkell has arranged."

Goda was young and could adapt herself to a new land, her children would have a birthplace and grow up according to its customs and its laws, and unless Edgar got himself killed in some foolish raid, there would be enough with the dowry she had insisted on giving the girl, some of the silver coins Eldred had left her, to buy a couple of fields. After a few months, there would be even no homesickness.

"But you cannot submit yourself to the Duke!" It must have been the tenth time that Edgar had repeated this but it was to allay his conscience. He knew, even better than Thorkell, that it would be disastrous if Elfleda sailed with them. She was too stern, too rigid, ever to live on easy terms with his companions or laugh, as Goda soon would, at their rougher, easier ways.

"Frain and Mildburh will take me in. I am an old widow and it may be that nobody will notice I have been away."

"Aboard! Aboard!" Most of the passengers had already gone out to the ships but the sailors wanted to give the young exiles as long a time as they could with a parent they were unlikely to see again. Besides, some of them had known Eldred and liked him.

"You must go. If I find life too difficult in Exeter, I'll come and join you in the North." It was a fable but it eased the parting.

"Aboard!" One of the men had seen the captain walking down the grass towards the beach. It was the final warning and Elfleda kissed the daughter who was, if she were honest with herself as she could not be at such a moment, already a stranger.

"Remember, our home is yours." Edgar meant the words as he said them although they would be forgotten as soon as his mother-in-law was out of sight. He took Goda by the arm, she was crying in spite of the vow she had made to be as impassive as her new countrymen, and pulled her towards the waiting coracle.

"Yes, Edgar, you were always loyal." The captain's footsteps scrunched over the shingle and the sailor shouted again. "Think of me sometimes," the wind was blowing her words away, "oh, Goda!"

The waves slapped the pebbles, the stones were the color of the sea but drier and flatter where the water had not touched them and further out, Goda was splashing almost up to her knees to reach the waiting craft. "Your kirtle, Goda, your new kirtle," Elfleda shouted a warning from force of habit as if the girl were still the ten year old child she had taken on summer feast days to the shore. If the captain had not stopped to talk to a friend, they would still be on the beach and he would have been angry; as it was, he hurried by without a glance. Custom required her to wait until her daughter was at the ship although Elfleda felt it would be easier to leave; farewells were harder the more they were prolonged. How gray, how choppy the sea was, the wind blew through her because her cloak had come unpinned and was flopping away from her shoulders but for the moment her mind was blank except for a memory of Goda running towards her on unsteady, infant legs, holding a poppy picked by the head. All that Goda had thought of then was to bring her a flower. How proud she had been of her! Why had she never imagined on that summer day that the years would separate them from each other? She had only thought of the continuity of life.

"You are wise." She had not noticed the Frisian come to her side, "We cannot transplant a tree, only a young bush."

"They have their lives to live." Everybody had said this to her during the last week but it was a phrase without a meaning.

"Osbern will be just to them and Edgar will soon settle down. He had always expected to be a farmer, remember."

"It is better for them to leave." What could strangers or even friends understand about her feelings? The coracle had not yet reached the *Spray* but all she could see was a blur, not much grayer than the waves.

"I know it is hard for you."

"It blots out the future." Thorkell felt her hatred of him rising as they stood together and yet what other future was there for the two young people? The hostility of the Irish was increasing day by day and he could not blame them for it when he saw the rapacity of the northern army. They were not exiles, these men had farms in their own country and had come simply for plunder.

"I know." He wondered as she walked away if he ought to accompany her or even (what did custom matter at such a time?) invite her to his hut? Exile had been the fortune of them all but she would answer as the rest had done, "Exeter was not your birthplace," as if a baby were aware of anything but his mother's arms? "It *is* my birthplace," he muttered, aware that nobody could hear him, it was beside the Exe that he had become conscious of himself and of gold and silver, though the gold was the marsh lilies and the silver, the river. It was where he had made his first voyage, a single day on a fishing boat one summer morning and where the sailors had talked to him about boundaries, not of walls and watchmen but shoals and fogs. It was to Exeter and to the house he had inherited from his father that he had returned after his journeys to feel the protection in winter of his own four walls. He had brought his charts and his movable possessions with him but what had happened to the ledge on which they had stood? Torn up for firewood probably just as the floors that had been so smooth under his rugs were now a mass of scratches from the nails in the soldiers' boots.

They were proud, the Exeter folk, they had taken his services and bargained against each other for his wares but they had never accepted him as a citizen, as one of themselves. Was he not as deeply hurt as Elfleda? She had lost her daughter, he the home that he had loved. He would go south in the spring to seek a place that would never remind him of Devon. There would be too many temptations to think about it if he remained in the seas round Flanders. His conscience pricked him and he hurried after Elfleda, she was standing with her face turned towards the land. "Come with me," he said almost roughly, "they cannot see us from so great a distance and we have a lot to discuss about your own journey. What is the use of watching the *Spray* sail out of sight of the harbor?"

XII

It had been too late in the season for a calm voyage and even some of the sailors had been seasick. Elfleda still lay on the straw in a little shelter they had arranged for her, although the sun was up and she ought to have gone to the bulwarks to look across at Exeter, if only from curiosity. It would have changed and she had changed and for a moment she wished herself back in the dank little Irish hut. It had been desolate, it had been foreign, but she had not had to relate her loneliness, her actual state, to the familiar surroundings of a happy childhood. Would Mildburh have forgotten her and Frain resent her coming because it would be, he must suppose, to claim the value of their abandoned house? How many hours she had spent during the last years trying to see the city in her mind, the blades of grass in the Duryard fields, the sedges in the marshes. Now the old fleece that a sailor had thrown over her, the crooked lines in a piece of timber near her head, her many fears, made an invisible net that held her more securely than iron fetters to this damp sleeping place aft of the mast. It was true that the captain had warned her not to show herself before the port reeve came on board but she could have stolen out and taken one look at the familiar waterside as the light quickened at dawn.

"No, just an old woman who was born here and wants to return to her kinsfolk," she heard voices along the deck.

"Another fugitive, I suppose."

"She seems to have been in Cornwall for many years."

"It's not that I blame a woman for leaving with her husband, it was her duty, but we want no foolish words added to the discontent over the castle."

"She's too old to trouble you, shall I fetch her?"

Perhaps it was as well that she had neither stirred nor combed out her hair but as the captain made a sign for her to follow him, she resented his words. She was not old. She had never seen the man who was tapping the bales laid out for his inspection but she knew the port reeve by sight. He had even waved goodbye to them when the *Seabird* had sailed. "Who are you?" he asked.

"Elfleda, daughter of Alwin." It was many years since her father had died and the name was a common one in the city. "My husband was in Master Ethelward's service," she mentioned the captain Thorkell had suggested, "and I went with him to Cornwall. After he died and my daughter married, I got lonely. I wanted to return to the city where I was born."

"When did you leave Exeter?"

"When?" She seemed to feel the Frisian at her shoulder as he had stood that day on the soft, green Irish turf, "Two, three, four," she counted on her fingers, "yes, it must be four years since my husband died and twenty since I left here."

"Then you were not in the city during the siege?" The reeve was looking at her so intently that she knew that he had recognized her.

"We lived high up the moors and all the news we heard was at the Michaelmas market."

The official continued to stare at her. She had on her worst dress, it was so old and patched she was about to throw it away when she had remembered what salt water could do to cloth. Her coif was stained with spilled broth and she must have looked yellow and wrinkled after having been seasick for several days, but old? No, she was not old. "She's an elderly woman," the captain repeated, "she can't do you any harm."

"But we don't want her falling on the bounty of the city. Have you still kinsfolk here?"

"I have several cousins." She did not want to implicate Mildburh if she could help it, she was not sure now that she wanted to remain.

The man hesitated and Elfleda kept her eyes on the board at her feet. "I shall not be a burden," she held out the smaller of her two purses, "my husband left me some silver when he died."

"And she has a bolt of cloth in the hold," the captain added quickly, "besides, at her age, what can she need?"

"I can still cook and spin if my cousins require my service."

"Very well, you may land, but look to your tongue.

We don't want trouble here, even if it is only a few fool-ish words from a kitchen corner."

"Thank you," she bowed humbly, where after all could she go if they turned her away?

"Get your things together," the captain ordered as curtly as if she had been a serving woman, "one of my men will help you to carry them ashore."

Elfleda bowed again, she caught a glimpse of the town as she turned, calm, peaceful, the grass more trampled than she remembered it when they had walked out on holidays to look at the anchored ships, but the general aspect was unchanged. Much had happened to her since she had left but painful as some of it had been, she would not have had it otherwise. Eldred had died, but she had been beside him, she had not to wake up from a night-mare wondering who had buried him on some distant battlefield. Goda had gone, but had she ever understood her daughter? She was so much a mixture of her spend-thrift, impulsive father and a cold caution that must have come to her from ancesters Elfleda had never known. Edgar, too, lived only for the moment, they were well matched. Now if she thought about those final months in Ireland, it was the Frisian who seemed to stand beside her. He had advised this return, he had found a passage for her, and all he asked in return was some word of his house. She combed her hair, put on a clean head cloth but it seemed wiser to land in her old dress. She was putting the last trifles into her bag when the captain called her. "Go quickly, before they change their minds. I sent a boy this morning to your kinsfolk, your cousin will be waiting inside the Gate."

"I am ready, but tell me," she asked the question in as

low a voice as possible, "have you heard yet what has happened to Thorkell's house?"

"There are Normans there and they have cut the trees down so as to have an uninterrupted view of the river, as if warships ever would sail up the Exe." He looked at her bag and motioned her to go; it was obvious that the reeve's questioning had made him uneasy and that he wanted to be rid of so dangerous a passenger at once.

"I am very grateful to you for your hospitality and kindness. If you see Thorkell at some port, please tell him that I got safely home."

Was Exeter really home? She followed the sailor who was carrying her possessions down a plank and onto the land. The fields looked the same, there were still a few late daisies in the corners where no feet had trampled them but something had gone from the landscape even if it was, as Mildburh said later, her imagination. The shock was too great and the words came to her lips that she had scolded the Saxons in the camp for saying too frequently, "What did we do wrong? Why did it have to happen to us?"

"Frain!" He looked older and thinner but when he laughed, opening his mouth very wide, he was still like one of Thorkell's monsters.

"So you've come back again?" He shook his head exactly as if she were a truant child.

"Eldred died, Goda married and I was alone."

"And then you remembered Exeter?"

"I thought of my kinsfolk. How is Mildburh? Is she well?"

"Very well. She does not know yet you are here. I was not sure when you would be able to leave the ship."

If you would be able to leave, Elfleda corrected him in her mind, he had been wondering if the port reeve would let her land and if this figure from the past would cause him trouble? His former liveliness had left him as it had never left the poor but independent group in Ireland. They looked at each other for a moment (was he sorry that she was here at all?), then he turned abruptly, motioning the sailor with her bales to follow them, "I expect you will notice many changes."

Yet it seemed the same at first. The street was familiar although the wattle fences needed repair and the gutters were choked with vegetable tops and refuse. She recognized the ledge where she had rested her pack while Eldred had tightened the straps and the little alleyway that was a short cut to the market. These had not altered although they had the shadowy grayness of a dream that slipped away as the sleeper woke.

"What has happened to the forge?" She wanted to be prepared before they turned the corner and had to pass in front of it.

"I did my best, Elfleda," there was a deep uneasiness under Frain's heartiness, "the property of the citizens who fled was confiscated."

Fled? What a strange word, the plunging ship, the fevers at the camp, even the grumbling loyalties, passed through her mind. They had still hoped then to save something of England.

"I had friends on the Council and they helped me. They knew I had been in favor of submission from the beginning. And I told them Eldred had been in debt to me." He was not excusing his opinions, he was proud of them. "I had to make many gifts but when they started pulling houses down . . ."

"To build the castle."

"Don't speak like that in the street," he glanced round but apart from an old man with a great, empty basket on his back, they were alone, "the families that were dispossessed needed homes and I saw it went to a friend of mine. He is paying for it gradually."

She had not expected to return to her own hearth but Frain seemed suddenly complacent and hard; not the kinsman who had carried Goda as a child on his shoulder or joked with them at feasts, but a stranger.

"You are welcome to a place in my household for as long as it pleases you," perhaps he was beginning to feel uneasy because much of what they had formerly owned must have passed into his hands while the *Seabird* was sailing down the river, "and you shall have a share from the yearly rent. But it cannot be much, there is the levy on the tribute and fines."

"I understand." It was fear, she decided, rather than unfriendliness that made him seem harsh to her. His freedom was limited and the Normans were his masters. It would be different with Mildburh and later on, if the situation proved too difficult, she had enough to find herself a room, either in Exeter or some neighboring village.

"It's an orderly city now the Godwins have gone."

She did not reply, they had come to Frain's house and she looked up at his apple tree, it was a trick she must remember if he tried to provoke her, "A fair crop, I see, in spite of the wet summer."

"Yes," he flung open the gate, "welcome home, we are glad to have you, kinswoman."

"And I am glad to be here."

Mildburh was looking down at the leeks, standing like housecarls stiffly in two rows, and was thankful to see no sign of slugs. She had not ripped out the rose bush but she had planted no flowers since the siege. The field was full of cows where the parley had been held but the harvest had been bad and the farmers were bringing little produce to the markets. Her husband had plenty of work but little to show for it. He mended harness and patched the leather coats that the formerly rich citizens now wore as cobbled as if they were churls but most of his gains went towards paying his share of the tribute.

"Mildburh!" She thought she heard her name but it was almost a whisper. It sounded like Elfleda's voice and she stooped over the leeks, cheered and yet sorrowful as she thought of her. She knew she would never see her friend again and she missed her.

"Mildburh!" This time she looked up. She might have mistaken in a crowded street the figure that was coming along the path for her former neighbor, although the lock of hair that was just showing under the hood was pure white. Elfleda! Had she stayed out in the sun too long but no, it was autumn and cold, it could not be a vision. Then she felt her friend's arms round her and knew that it was her voice. "Eldred died, Mildburh, so I've come back to Exeter."

"And I never thought to see you again." She stood back, remembering their parting that last dreadful day of the siege. Yes, it was no phantom, it was Elfleda, though there were many more wrinkles now in the familiar face.

"He died from a fever," Elfleda repeated, "in Ireland."

"He ought never to have left."

"He was loyal to the mother of his lord. Besides, the Normans here would have killed him."

"He was loyal to his lord but not to his family."

"Yes, in his way, he was loyal to us all. After his death, Goda married that thane's son from Sussex and they sailed north. They asked me to go with them but I could not change lands a third time. I missed my city."

"You should never have left us."

"It was my duty. At least I was with Eldred when he died and the Godwin standard was flying above the camp."

"Oh, never use that word unless you are sure we are alone," Mildburh looked round the garden anxiously to make sure no neighbor had overheard them.

"I will be careful once I have told you my story." The hut in Ireland had smelled of moss and smoke but she had been free.

"Frain sold the forge," Mildburh said awkwardly, "we feared it would be confiscated and we should have Normans as neighbors."

"What should I do alone in that big house?" She did not add what she was thinking, memories would drive her out of it into the woods. "No, Goda had her dowry but I still have enough to find a room somewhere and live in it till I die."

"There's our attic. But it would not be fit for you."
The Christmas feasts, the plenty in Elfleda's house and in
particular a brace of ducks that she had once served,
made Mildburh hungry whenever she remembered them.
"It's warm but it's a servant's room."

"I was hoping on the ship that you would offer it to
me. I can help you with the garden and they used to
praise my spinning. Besides, I brought enough to pay a
little if you take me into your household and Frain says
he owes me something for the house."

"How times have changed!" They were lucky now if
they could afford an extra joint or a small cake when the
festivals came round. Their masters kept the hunting
along the marshes for themselves. "Yes, it isn't as if you
were a man . . ." Mildburh broke off her sentence in
shame, what had the years done to her to make her put
her kinswoman second to her own safety?

"You mean they would have banished Eldred but an
old woman, not dependent on their charity, can be ignored?"

"Not ignored, Elfleda, loved." Mildburh took her by
the arm and they walked side by side into the kitchen
where her own spinning wheel was standing in the corner and it was just different enough from her former
home to make her return bearable.

The attic was pleasantly warm. It still smelled of last
year's apples although the new crop was almost ripe. It
sloped, it would take her a day or two to avoid striking
her head against a beam if she moved hurriedly but she
would be the first in the house to hear the birds and

watch light coming through the crevices of the thatch. On bitter winter nights, Mildburh had insisted, she must sleep below in the kitchen. Her bales were stacked in a corner, she had hung her cloak on a peg in the wall. She unpacked the bag that she had carried herself, it contained little but the dusty kerchief that she had worn during the journey and that she must ask permission to wash the next day, a comb, a cup, a phial of feverfew wrapped in a tattered skirt that it had seemed wasteful to leave behind and a small, gray pebble (she wondered now why she had brought it) from Eldred's tomb on the cliffs. She was home. She felt almost happy as she heard the shouts warning citizens to go to their beds. "A candle?" Mildburh had offered it as a favor but she had refused. "I shall sleep at once tonight. The last week I kept wondering if the ship would capsize and if we should ever reach port."

A flicker of light, perhaps from some wayfarer's torch, still came faintly through a hole (she must find some straw and block it up in the morning) yet though the perils were over, those violent waves smashing from bow to stern, that grim anxiety as to whether they would let her through the Gate, she felt as she hung her dress beside her cloak that besides being the end of her journey, it was also the finish of her life. She regretted nothing, she wanted nothing. Unlikely things happened because she had never expected to return to Exeter, but she would also never walk again to Eldred's grave and it was doubtful if she would ever hear news of her daughter. Destiny was harsh, harsh . . . she scratched the thatch above her head and a sack of dried camomile (she had always

kept hers in the shed) made her cough. She poked her
finger through the hole, no, she would not stop it up because of the draft, she wanted to feel the air, the soft,
Devon air that she had breathed at birth. The thatch tore
more than she meant although it was little wider than
the point of a blunt awl and she stared through it as a hare
might peer from a bush inside the forest. Winter was
ahead when people would break off a tale, remember, and
gaze moodily into the fire. What could she do but wait,
as patiently as she was able, it was the exile's lesson, till
she could follow Eldred on his journey? If this had happened . . . or that . . . she tore the hole wider and
tried to look up into a night without stars, wondering
idly and completely without fear, what there could be on
the other side of the darkness?